A PARKER SPOONER MYSTERY

VOICES OF THE DOLPHINS

A NOVEL BY PHILIP LEHPAMER

Philip Lehpamer is a retired life insurance actuary, a retired fellow of the Society of the Actuaries, and a member of the American Academy of Actuaries. He has lived and worked most of his life in New York; however, his fictional actuary and private investigator, Parker Spooner, lives and works in Chicago where Mr. Lehpamer was born and went to school. It was after the Covid years that Mr. Lehpamer turned to writing and places his characters in Chicago during the 1970's.

All characters in this novel are fictional except for historically named and recognized chess players and well-known religious figures. Any other possible reference to a real person is purely coincidental and not intentional.

ISBN: 978-1-972919-00-2

Boulevard Books

The New Face of Publishing

This novel is dedicated to all chess players, especially those who may have come to the game during the summer of 1972.

A PARKER SPOONER MYSTERY

VOICES OF THE DOLPHINS

PHILIP LEHPAMER

(1) Oscar Busby is Dead

Oscar Busby had been found with his throat cut, quite dead, on his kitchen floor by the landlady when she entered his Chicago apartment on the morning of Thursday, June 1, 1972. There was no murder weapon on the blood-coated floor, only Oscar's body. Mrs. Murray screamed, turned, and ran down the stairs to her apartment. Her husband, John Murray, having heard her scream, had just jumped out of his bed and was still in his underwear as he opened their apartment door.

"What's wrong, Ruthy?" he cried as she ran past him into to their bedroom and grabbed the telephone that rested on a nightstand.

"Get me the police! There's been a murder." she yelled into the phone to the operator.

And that's how Detective Sergeant Michael Boyle of the Area 6 Homicide unit located on Damen Avenue as part of Chicago's 19th Police District wound up with a new murder to solve. He and his police officers spent the remainder of day questioning the Murray's and combing through Busby's apartment looking for clues and evidence as to what may have happened overnight in that two-family building in the New Town section of Chicago.

Sergeant Boyle knew about Oscar from his son-in-law, Parker Spooner. Parker ran his own actuarial consulting firm and had been trained by the Sergeant as a private investigator. As such, the two sometimes collaborated on murder investigations. The most recent were two separate murders that came together, and which were documented in *Unwavering Love*. Thus, Sergeant Boyle decided that he would visit Parker and inform him about the murder of Oscar Busby.

Meanwhile, while all this was happening, Father Joseph, a Roman Catholic priest was saying mass at St. Thomas the Apostle Church in the Hyde Park section of Chicago where Parker and his family worshipped. The gospel for that day was from Matthew, chapter 6, verses 7-15, and Father Joseph read using the words from the New American Bible, which had just been published in July 1970 by the Catholic Book Publishing Company: "In your prayer, do not rattle on like the pagans. They think they will win a hearing by the sheer multiplication of words. Do not imitate them. Your Father knows what you need before you ask him. This is how you are to pray. 'Our Father in heaven, hallowed be your name, your kingdom come, your will be done on earth as it is in heaven. Give us today our daily bread and forgive us the wrong we have done as we forgive those who wrong us. Subject us not to the trial but deliver us from the evil one.' If you forgive the faults of others, your heavenly Father will forgive you yours. If you do not forgive others, neither will your Father forgive you."

In his homily, Father Joseph said this prayer, the Our Father was probably the most famous Christian prayer and was likely recited at least once a week by all Christian denominations. He called upon his parishioners to think about this prayer and then to forgive the faults of their neighbors.

Father Joseph finished mass and went on with his daily routine of running a parish. He was not aware of Oscar Busby's murder and did not even know the man, but eventually with the passage of time, Oscar's murder would have an indirect impact on his parishioners because Oscar was a spy for the United States Central Intelligence Agency and his murder would set off a ripple of waves that would lead to arrests and reveal a secret that to this day is kept quiet and generally not known.

But all of that was in the future, and we now return to the spring evening of June 1, 1972, when Sergeant Boyle went to Parker's house in the Hyde Park section of Chicago to talk to his son-in-law about the death of Oscar Busby. The Sergeant was greeted by his daughter, Rosemary, Parker's wife, and then by the two youngest children, 12-year-old Peter and 6-year-old Anna, both of whom were excited at Grandpa's unexpected visit.

"Dad, what brings you here tonight?" asked Rosemary as the grandkids bounced around him.

"I have to talk to Parker about a mutual acquaintance," replied the Sergeant quietly.

At that moment, Parker with big smile greeted his father-in-law, "Dad, it's great to see you!" and the two men warmly hugged each other.

This commotion created by the Sergeant's arrival alerted 17-year-old Grace, the older daughter, and John, their 19-year-old eldest son, to come out of their upstairs bedrooms and run down the stairs to greet their grandpa. Grace was graduating from high school in ten days and excited about joining John in September at the University of Chicago where her brother was finishing his freshman year. Parker was a Chicago graduate himself having majored in mathematics in the late 1940's and pleased that his two oldest children had been admitted to his college where John was studying physics while Grace would be studying English literature.

After chatting briefly with the family, Parker took his father-in-law into the den and closed the door, pouring a 7 up for each of them.

"What's going on, Dad? What brings you here on a Thursday night?" asked Parker after the two men had settled into comfortable chairs facing each other.

"Unfortunately, Parker, I have bad news. One of the chess players you know at the Gompers Park site, Oscar Busby, was murdered last night in his apartment. His throat was cut with a knife that the killer apparently owned because only the body was on the kitchen floor and there was no knife anywhere around the murder scene, either inside or outside the house."

Parker was surprised and asked, "Oscar Busby murdered - any idea who killed him?"

"No suspects as yet, however, besides Oscar's fingerprints we found another set in the apartment. Based on what the landlord has told us, they may belong to his girlfriend, Susan Danford, but so far we haven't been able to locate her. Anyway, I'm here to show you something that was found on Oscar, and I hope you can give me some information about the numbers I'll be showing you."

Parker nodded, "I've known Oscar about a year and that only happened because Peter developed an interest in chess, and I started taking him to the Gompers Park Chess Club. That's where I met Oscar who's a regular there, and a very good player but nowhere near being a master. Nevertheless, everybody at the Gompers Park chess club knows him. He also was a race track fan and took bets on races and other sporting events. I've seen him exchanging money with other chess players and writing in a small black book that he kept in his coat pocket."

"I've heard about Oscar's interest in horse racing from John Murray, his landlord," replied the Sergeant. "Busby tried to involve him in betting on horse races, but John told him he wasn't interested, and Oscar never bothered his landlord again. Both John and his wife, Ruthy, also mentioned Oscar's black book. Unfortunately, the book wasn't on him, and thus far, we haven't found it among his belongings. Perhaps the killer took it after the murder, but we'll continue to search for his black book to see if it holds any clues."

Parker nodded, "I never knew what Oscar did for a living. It didn't seem like he had a job."

"One of the things we did find on Oscar was this piece of paper," said Sergeant Michael handing it to Parker. The paper had been twice folded but was now flat. Parker took it and printed in large capitals was the note – LOOK TO COLLECT ALL MONEY BY ELEVEN - Parker looked at his father-in-law who continued, "I'm showing you this because I want you, a life insurance actuary, to see what's on the back and explain it to me."

Parker turned the paper over and immediately recognized the start of a standard life insurance mortality table. He moved next to his father-in-law and raised the paper to eye level so that both of them could view it together.

The Commissioners 1958 Standard Ordinary (1958 CSO) Mortality Table (Male Lives):

x	lx	dx	1000qx
0	10,000,000	70,800	7.08
1	9,929,200	17,475	1.76
2	9,911,725	15,066	1.52
3	9,896,659	14,449	1.46

"This is the first four rows of a male mortality table to value life insurance policies," said Parker. "Ages 4 through 99 are not shown but the first column headed by the letter x represents the age of the individual starting at birth or age 0 and then ages 1, 2, and 3. The next column is labeled lx and represents the number of lives at each age starting with a hypothetical 10 million births at age 0 and working down to 9,896,659 at age 3. The third column is label dx and represents the number of deaths, which in the first year of life is 70,800. The number of deaths at age 3 is 14,449 deaths. Finally, the last column is the mortality rate at each age. It starts at 7.08 per 1,000 males in the first year of life and drops to 1.46 per 1,000 males at age 3. Such a mortality table is used for valuation purposes in the insurance industry and not for any other reason."

"So an insurance agent wouldn't be carrying this around since it doesn't represent the premium charged for the policy?" replied Sergeant Boyle, looking at the insurance table.

"That's right," replied Parker. "This table would be familiar to life insurance actuaries or to regulators in the various State Insurance Departments who monitor insurance companies."

"Ok," replied Sergeant Boyle, "so the note printed on the other side of this paper asking for money was not a request for an insurance payment. I wonder if the person who wrote the note even knew that these numbers were on the other side of the paper. This piece of paper was found folded in the pocket of the victim, and the mortality table was not visible."

"It's possible that the person who wrote the message didn't know that there was this mortality table on the other side of the paper," reflected Parker, "but it's also possible that the person didn't care what was written on the other side." "That could be," replied the Sergeant, "but it's also strange to me that the note is printed in block capitals. Normally, a person would write a note, not print it, but let's say that if you had bad handwriting, then printing the note would make sense. But why would every letter be capitalized?"

"Perhaps the person printing this note wanted to emphasize the entire message," ventured Parker.

"Okay, son-in-law," replied a smiling Michael Boyle, "but whatever the situation is, I hope this note is going to involve you as an actuary in this murder investigation because of the table on the back."

Now it was Parker's turn to smile. Yes, he was a life insurance actuary, a fellow of the Society of Actuaries (FSA) and as such had knowledge of various risks in forming life insurance products such as longevity risks, interest rate risks, inflation risks along with investment risks. He had formed his own insurance consulting firm right around the time that his father-in-law, Sergeant Michael Boyle, started training him and getting Parker involved in detective work that aided the police. One of the main reasons for Parker's involvement was that he was known to have sudden "insights" which allowed him to solve cases. Whether his insights were chance, psychic, religious, quantum or some combination of those forces or something entirely else, Parker had developed a solid reputation for connecting people and events and solving difficult police investigations because of those unexpected insights. Thus, on this day in late spring, the day after Oscar Busby was murdered in his kitchen, and the message LOOK TO COLLECT ALL MONEY BY ELEVEN was found, Parker suddenly knew that his father-in-law was correct and that he was going to be involved in solving Oscar Busby's murder, but at that moment Parker didn't know anything about the case or what the message in bold capital letters meant. Nevertheless, Parker nodded his assent to help the Sergeant and his police find the person who murdered Oscar Busby.

"Parker," said the Sergeant, "I'm going to be visiting the Gompers Park Chess Club tomorrow night to talk to the players about Oscar and perhaps find some clues regarding his murder. Since you're a club member, I'm wondering if you'll be there?"

"Yes, Dad, tomorrow is a Friday night, and the place will be full as the club has many chess players. Your grandson, Peter, will want to go to play chess, and I'll drive him there and take him home. I'll be very happy to have you there and will introduce you to the players I know at the Gompers Park Chess Club."

(2) A Night at Gompers Park

In 1972 the chess world was in a frenzy. The on and off match between the current world champion, Boris Spassky, representing the Soviet Union, and Bobby Fischer from the United States was still on according to the June issue of the American monthly magazine Chess Life & Review. The magazine also wrote that most players thought that Bobby would take the title from Boris and break the decades old strangle-hold that the Soviets had on the royal game.

The upcoming chess match was the main topic of discussion that occurred at the Gompers Park Chess Club that Friday night in early June 1972; however, very quietly and quickly, the news of Oscar's murder circulated among the chess players, bringing initial disbelief followed by stunned speculation as to what happened. 'He was doing business with the mob, and they didn't like the bets that he made' was a typical comment that was made based on unfounded wild speculations.

Detective Sergeant Michael Boyle heard some of these speculations as he circulated around the Club that evening with his son-in-law, Parker Spooner. The Sergeant was not in uniform, and players called him Michael even though many of the chess players at Gompers Park knew he was a police detective. Parker managed to pull three chess players away from their games to join him along with Michael in a side room. Kyle and Lev were friends for years and both enjoyed the royal game. They sat next to each other on a sofa in front of a glass coffee table while Parker and Michael took seats on the other sofa opposite them. Jackson, the third chess player, who was well into his seventies, knew everyone at the club, and was there not only to play chess but to talk. He joined the group around the table, sitting on a single sofa that also had a note pad and pencil.

"Oscar's death is shocking but I did warn him that he was playing with fire associating with the Glueck brothers," said Jackson shaking his head sadly.

"Who are the Glueck brothers?" questioned Parker.

"Their father was a mobster and served time in the early forties and died in prison. The mother did the best she could to raise her kids but got sick and died leaving two sons when they were ages 18 and 20. Soon thereafter, the brothers went off the rails and became younger versions of their father. I don't know how Oscar ever got mixed up with them, but he did, and now this terrible murder - just horrible," said Jackson.

"In what way have the Glueck brothers gone wrong?" probed Parker.

"They sell jewelry, in particular diamond rings and emeralds, and many times they're fake jewels. The diamonds aren't real."

Here Michael nodded agreement, "It's not my Department but I've heard similar things from other policemen. Apparently many of the men who bought fake diamond rings for their upcoming weddings didn't file a complaint because they were embarrassed by their mistake, and there was no need to do so since their ladies weren't aware of the fake diamond and happy that they finally had an engagement ring. The handful who did file complaints exchanged their fakes for real diamonds when the Glueck's said they were unaware of the fakes, made the changes, and were never arrested."

“Are the Glueck brothers members of this chess club?” asked Parker.

“No, and I don’t know if they play chess, but the few times I’ve been to Arlington Race Track, I’ve seen them there,” replied Jackson.

Kyle and Lev smiled, and Kyle said, “David Glueck is a very big, muscle bound, guy. His younger brother, Donald Glueck, is not as big but neither one looks like the typical chess player, but of course, as the saying goes, one shouldn’t judge a book by its cover.”

Lev then said, “Both of these brothers drive luxury cars and are into jewels, and I don’t think chess is of interest to them because there just isn’t that much money in chess even though Fischer is asking for more money and thus delaying the start of his match with Spassky.”

Michael, concerned that the discussion would drift into chess, learned forward and bluntly asked, “Do any of you gentlemen have any idea why someone would want Oscar dead?”

With that question, both Kyle and Lev looked at each other and then shook their heads with a collective no. After a long pause, Jackson offered, “I haven’t seen Oscar’s girlfriend in several weeks. Susan Danford used to come with Oscar to the Club and play different opponents. Good looking woman, smart, and not a bad player. Last week I asked Oscar about Susan, and he told me she was angry at him. He then walked away, not wanting to talk about her. My guess is that she wanted to get married and he wasn’t asking her, and they had a bad argument.”

“I also haven’t seen Susan in some time,” said Kyle, “but I can’t believe she would murder Oscar even if they argued and he wouldn’t marry her.”

“But a woman scorned could lose control, and scorned love could turn to hate in a desperate moment,” countered Lev.

Jackson quickly shook his head no. “I agree with Kyle. Susan’s not a person who would murder Oscar. Even if Oscar told her that he would never marry her, she might cry and never come back to Gompers Park, but she wouldn’t kill him – she would just leave him. Susan’s a smart self-sufficient woman who has money.”

With that, the three men – Kyle, Lev, and Jackson looked at Parker who smiled and said,
“I don’t know Susan. I’ve seen her here at the club once but never talked to her. Some people do lose control, but a woman cutting a man’s throat in a moment of desperation seems to me to be highly unusual. Yet sometimes people do terrible things.”

At that moment, Parker glanced at Michael, and the Sergeant gave him a look and a quick wink that indicated that his police had already located Susan Danford and had arranged to talk to her about Oscar’s murder. Michael then stopped asking questions and said to the group, “I think Oscar was involved in other things besides chess, and I would appreciate your input as to what Oscar was doing at this Chess Club besides playing chess.”

The three men glanced at each other and then Jackson offered, “Oscar was a gambler and a bookie – yes, making book was his work. That’s what he did for a living and many of our club members used him to bet on sporting activities. I didn’t think there was anything out of order with him up to a few weeks ago when suddenly Oscar became quiet and more inward."

Kyle and Lev nodded agreement, and Lev added, "Oscar and Susan went on vacation to Florida for a week in April, and I noticed the change when he returned. Something must have happened to them down there."

"I agree," said Kyle, "and it was after their trip that Susan stopped coming to the Club."

"Jackson, what kind of gambling was Oscar involved with?" asked Sergeant Michael Boyle.

"Oscar would take bets on anything, including the big events. We had the Kentucky Debry and the Preakness in May and now the Belmont is coming up. The Indy 500 just happened last Saturday, and people have been placing bets on who will win the American and National League and the World Series, who's the best pitcher, hitter, you name it and Oscar will take a bet on anything you want."

"He had no middle man to help him take and pay out bets?"

"Not that I heard of or ever saw – he worked by himself, but he talked to everyone at the Club, and certainly a couple of guys gave him information that Oscar used to set the bets," replied Jackson.

"Can you share with me who at the club used his services the most or may have helped him in that way?" asked the Sergeant.

"Bob Hanson, but he's not around tonight, which is strange because he never misses a Friday. However, Frank Costello is here tonight as is Barry Snyder and both of them are big sport fans and help manage Club tournaments and events. I'm thinking these guys helped Oscar set bets by using their knowledge and talking sports with him."

"I'll talk to Frank and Barry tonight before I leave. Would you have Bob Hanson home address and phone number?

Jackson reached down to the pad of paper and pencil on the table and started writing, "This address is for a duplex, a two-family house. Bob lives upstairs."

Michael looked at what had been written and placed the paper in his shirt pocket, "Thank you, Jackson, and this change you noticed in Oscar – when he first became quiet or inward dealing with his clients - this change happened after he returned from his recent Florida trip – is that correct?"

Jackson nodded yes, followed by agreeing nods from Kyle and Lev.

"Well, thank you, gentlemen, thank you for your comments – that does give me a place to start," said Sergeant Boyle, shaking the hands goodbye of the three men as they exited the room.

"So what else have you learned?" asked Parker after he and Michael were alone in the room.

"Everyone I spoke to agrees that Oscar was a gambler, that's what he did with his life and time. Then something went wrong with a recent trip he took to Florida. He and his girlfriend have separated, and this has impacted his style."

"Were you able to talk to his girlfriend, Susan Danford?"

"Yes, we went to her apartment this morning. She confirmed that Oscar broke their arrangement after she pressed him for marriage as they vacationed in Florida. She cried at the news of his death, but she's an independent, smart woman with plenty of money, and she's not sitting around mourning. We asked her to the Area 6 homicide office for a detailed interview. If you're not doing anything tomorrow around 1 pm, you're invited to join us, Parker. But for now, I want to button hole Frank Costello and Barry Snyder. Please wait here, and I'll find and bring them over one at a time to hear what they have to say."

Parker nodded and waited. A few minutes later Sergeant Boyle returned followed by a small bald headed man wearing a suit and tie who looked worried. "Parker, do you know, Barry Snyder?" asked the Sergeant.

"I know he is one of the mainstays of the Chess Club," said Parker, "but I never had the pleasure of meeting him." The two men shook hands.

"It's good meeting you, Parker, and it's great that you're bringing your young son, Peter, to our Club. He's a very good, logical player and has already made an impression on us at age 12. I hope you take him to a United States Chess Federation tournament soon so he can get a USCF rating. I think someday he will be a chess master if he studies and plays in tournaments."

"Thank you, Barry. Peter has many interests, including basketball, and he's growing tall quickly so we'll see what happens in the next school year when he enters 7th grade and can play on his school's basketball team."

"Yea," said Barry sadly but then getting excited, "We lose so many kids to major sports, but after Fischer beats

Spassky and wins the World Chess Championship this summer, I think the game we love is going to explode in the United States."

"I hope the match gets played," responded Parker. "Apparently, there's a lot of drama going on behind the scenes about Fischer's demands."

"Fischer will play because he wants to be World Champion," said Barry with conviction, adding "I have a number of Russian friends, and they say Russian domination of chess is over."

In order to get the conversation away from chess and back to his issue Sergeant Boyle quickly asked, "Mr. Snyder, I suspect all your Club members are shocked by the murder of Oscar Busby. Is there anything or anybody that comes to mind as to why or who could have committed this crime? Sometimes the smallest hint can start a successful police investigation."

"Well, of course, there are the Glueck brothers," said Snyder. "They don't play chess, but Oscar took bets from them and perhaps big ones. If Oscar lost one of those bets and didn't have the money to pay the brothers, I wouldn't want to be him. Those guys have a nasty reputation."

"Okay, is there anybody else? Do any other individuals come to mind?" asked the Sergeant.

"Not really, there's nobody in this Club who would kill Oscar over some bets."

With that Sergeant Boyle thanked Barry Snyder who left the room. A few minutes later the Sergeant had Frank Costello with him, and the scene was replayed as Frank also mentioned the Glueck brothers as possible suspects and also thought none of the Gompers Park chess players were capable of murdering anyone, let alone Oscar.

Parker shrugged his shoulders and merely smiled at the Sergeant that the consensus of these two chess players was that no chess player would ever murder anyone. "See you tomorrow, Dad, for the Susan Danford interview," and with that Parker waved good-bye to his father-in-law.

Parker found his son Peter immersed in a chess game with plenty of time on each player's clock. With this chess game going, Parker knew he wasn't getting out of the Gompers Park Club anytime soon and pulled up a chair to watch. Peter had the white pieces and was playing Pavel Kotov, an established solid class A chess player. Peter had a spatial advantage on the king side, but Pavel had just made a move to trade off Peter's bishop that was pinning Pavel's knight. Peter had choices including taking the knight or withdrawing his bishop. However, Peter's move was a surprising sacrifice of his bishop as he pushed his rook pawn and after his bishop was taken, Peter's rook pawn captured the black pawn and opened Peter's rook to attack black's king. Unfortunately, this was not a sound sacrifice and a few moves later Peter's attack fizzled and being down a bishop without compensation, Peter extended his hand and resigned.

"I was too aggressive sacrificing my bishop," said Peter.

"Yes, the positions are equal if you take knight with your bishop," replied Pavel, who was an elderly middle-aged man with a slight Russian accent.

Peter looked disappointed, and Parker hugged his son, "You learned something tonight, Peter. Just remember how this position unfolded for future games and you'll do better next time." The father and son drove back to their Hyde Park home talking about chess. Parker was happy that Peter enjoyed playing the game and also happy for himself that he was going to help his father-in-law, a Chicago police detective who ran Area Six homicide, solve a murder.

(3) Susan Danford's Interview

The next day Parker arrived early at Chicago's Area Six police station on Damen Avenue, which no one could miss because the three-story building had the words Police Station written in large letters above the door. Inside, he was greeted by Detective Brendan, who Parker had worked with before. Brendan was the detective's first name and that's how he wanted to be called because his last name was difficult if not impossible to pronounce correctly, being a long hyphenated African Irish Gaelic combination. Detective Brendan stood 6 feet, 3 inches tall, was muscular, and had a black, pockmarked face that instinctively told everyone not to mess with him. However, everyone who knew this detective recognized that he had a heart of gold if you were honest with him.

Parker and Detective Brendan warmly greeted each other and then walked up to the third floor using the dilapidated stairs in a no elevator building that was falling apart. There the Homicide Unit worked, and Sergeant Boyle waited. "Miss Danford called to say she was on her way," said Sergeant Michael Boyle as he rearranged stacks of paper on his desk. Within minutes, Susan Danford, following a clerk, came up the stairs and took a chair in front of the Sergeant's desk. She was a bleached blonde with a young face and a youthful figure to match. She was expensively dressed and had an air of independence showing she wasn't lacking money. Parker had seen her before on a Friday night when she and Oscar were playing chess at the Gompers Park site. The Sergeant introduced Detective Brendan and then Parker, saying to Susan that Parker Spooner was not a policeman but did assist the police and a person who might be helpful since he knew many Gompers Park chess players.

"Oh, yes, I recognize you from the Club. You have a young son, Peter, who comes with you," said Susan smiling and shaking Parker's extended hand.

"Yes, Peter's excited about chess and now nearly everyone in the United States knows Bobby Fischer, and that's the reason I've been going to the Gompers Park site."

The four of them then sat around a table, and Sergeant Boyle started by asking Miss Danford, "When and how did you and Oscar Busby meet?"

"It was last New Year's Eve at a party in a house of a mutual friend. We started talking and at midnight he gave me a long kiss and asked me out. We started dating in early January," replied Susan, who then started crying. She grabbed a hanky from her purse and quickly pulled herself together. "We broke up in April after a Florida vacation where it became clear that a marriage wasn't going to happen."

"Would you be willing to talk about him and your break up, Miss Danford? It might give us a lead as to who killed him."

"Yes, I'll talk about Oscar – that's why I'm here." She took a deep breath and started, "Oscar and I got along very well at first even though he was twenty plus years older than me. He was into betting on everything and had dozens of people who placed bets with him. Every afternoon he would be on the phone making bets and recording the information in his black book. I had never met anyone like him. He was completely fascinating the way he talked on the phone being very quick and smart to do all those mental calculations and to establish the odds he quoted. Then later he would go out with his black book to collect from the losers and pay off the winners."

"Was there anyone in particular that he mentioned or that you met during this time?" asked Boyle.

"I never really met that many of his clients. However, some of the chess players at Gompers Park like Frank Costello, Barry Snyder, and especially Bob Hanson were guys who were close to him at the Club and helped him evaluate races and teams," replied Susan.

"Did anything unusual happen or does anything come to mind with any of these men and Oscar? Perhaps there was a minor disagreement with Oscar over their dealings. Then again perhaps only one of them was involved, or was there some incident that upset their dealings with Oscar?"

"No, I didn't see or hear anything like that. They all seemed to get along and were friends."

"You mentioned Oscar kept records in a black book. We didn't find any records or black books in his apartment."

Susan took a long pause as if she was debating how to answer but finally said, "Oscar would burn the book once the pages were full. I saw him throw the last one into a coal furnace. His current black book was always with him. He literally slept with it." Susan paused and then added, "If you couldn't find it on him, then his killer probably took it."

"Interesting," said the Sergeant, "he would burn his old records. Could you give me the location of the furnace where he got rid of his prior book?

"It's in the basement of the two family where he lived. That's the house that John and Ruthy Murray own."

"When did Oscar throw his prior black book into their furnace?"

"It was sometime in April, right before our trip to Florida," replied Susan.

"Ok, so there's some small chance that the furnace hasn't been used since we're well into spring; however, some nights in late April can be chilly if not cold," said the Sergeant. Turning to Detective Brendan, he continued, "I would like you to go to the Murray's house and retrieve Oscar's prior black book from their coal furnace, assuming it hasn't been consumed by fire. Parker, would you go with Detective Brendan and if any part of the black book exists and is readable, I'd like you to examine it and tell me what you find. It should have dates and dollar bets along with payoffs. The murderer may have been placing bets with Oscar, and the name would be there if we could somehow figure it out. Being an actuary, you're a whiz with numbers, and you may be able to sort it out, especially if there are large bets or if something looks strange." Both Detective Brendan and Parker smiled at all of this and said yes to the Sergeant's requests.

With those commands out of the way, the Sergeant felt he might be making progress and turned to Susan, "Besides the Chess Club, did Oscar have other friends or associates? Do you have any ideas as to who might have killed him or wanted him dead?"

"Not really. I know he was wary of the Glueck brothers, but he still took their money and sometimes their jewelry in place of money when they placed bets with him."

"I'm aware that the Glueck brothers are jewelers," said Boyle, "but surprised that Oscar would take jewelry in lieu of money."

"Oscar gave me a bracelet in March and a pair of earrings in April," replied Susan, who had plenty of money herself but gladly accepted Oscar's gifts.

"Interesting," said the Sergeant as the case seemed to be developing some unique features. "What about Oscar's family or some of his other friends and associates?"

"Oscar was an only child and had no family. I briefly met some of his friends or associates when we took a trip to Florida, but he kept most of that to himself and didn't want to talk about it. Our Florida trip at the end of April was the cause of our breakup."

Sergeant Boyle took note and quickly said, "We are almost done with this interview, and I thank you, Miss Danford, for cooperating and being candid with us. Before you go, I would like to ask you a couple of personal questions, which you just alluded to. In particular, you said initially that Oscar and you got along. Would you share with me what caused you to separate?"

Susan looked at him and didn't hesitate, "By early April, I was bored with his routine. I knew how he did the odds and his system. He seemed perfectly happy doing this stuff day after day. I hoped our planned vacation to Miami in April would change the situation, but it made it worse. While there, he got telephone calls from some guy called Boris Volkov, who had a terrible Russian accent. Oscar would go out in the evenings, saying he would right back, but that wasn't the case; he was always back late, and he wouldn't talk to me about it. The third time it happened, I followed him out of the motel and saw him get into a white Mercedes driven by a beautiful woman with flowing blonde golden hair. That did it for me. I confronted him when he returned. I wanted to know what he was up to, and I again mentioned marriage to him. We had an argument. Oscar said I should stay out of things that I didn't understand and that he couldn't talk about. I didn't understand that. We returned to Chicago and separated for good. I told him I wouldn't be his mistress."

With that, Susan Danford started to cry, and the interview paused. Detective Brendan sat and spoke softly to her, while Sergeant Boyle and Parker exited the room to talk. The Sergeant updated Parker, "Out of the three names that Susan mentioned, we've already talked to Frank Costello and Barry Snyder. Frank knows both horse and car racing very well and gave information to Oscar that helped him set odds. Barry knew the major sports, helping Oscar to set odds on baseball, football, basketball, and hockey games. I suspect that Bob Hanson did the same thing for soccer, tennis, and golf; however, we cannot locate him. This morning his landlady told Detective Brendan that Bob packed two bag early Friday morning – that's just a few hours after the murder - and left for parts unknown. The landlady also said Hanson wasn't certain when he would be back, but she would contact us when he returned. We obviously need to locate Bob Hanson and based on what Susan just said, we have to find out what Oscar was doing in Miami last April."

The two men reentered the room. Susan had stopped crying, and Sergeant Boyle asked her, "There's a set of unidentified fingerprints in Oscar's kitchen. Would you allow us to take your fingerprints?"

Susan hesitated as if she was confused or undecided, keeping her eyes down, but then responded, in a halting voice, "I haven't been in Oscar's kitchen in weeks. I don't think they could be mine."

"Probably not, but if fresh prints are there, you would be a likely suspect," said the smiling Sergeant.

"Go ahead and take them. I have nothing to hide," replied a suddenly defiant Susan, looking up at the Sergeant.

Sergeant Boyle nodded, "Detective Brendan, please take Miss Danford's fingerprints."

"Follow me," said the detective, standing up and motioning to Susan, who followed him to another desk at the far end of the third floor. The fingerprinting process went quickly, and Susan returned with Detective Brendan to the Sergeant's desk.

Once she was settled, Sergeant Boyle asked, "I have one more question where you may be able to help me in this investigation of Oscar's murder and that concerns Bob Hanson."

"Bob's a really nice guy. He and Oscar were friends," replied Susan smiling and perking up noticeably when she mentioned Bob's name. "What's your question?"

"Bob apparently left Chicago early Friday morning according to his landlady, and she doesn't know where he went or when he will return. He wasn't at the chess club last night, and we would like to talk to him. Do you have any idea where he may be?"

"No, I haven't seen Bob since I stopped going to the Club, and I don't really know much about him. I always thought that he and Oscar were kind of close although Oscar never talked about anyone. My guess is that Bob went on a vacation somewhere and doesn't know about the murder."

"Why do you think that Oscar and Bob were kind of close?" asked the Seargent.

"When Oscar and I went to parties, Bob was usually there, and he and Oscar would usually spend time together talking about something by themselves, just the two of them off in some corner."

"Oscar never said anything to you about Bob or their conversations?"

"No, never, and I never asked," replied Susan. "I hope you find Bob and that he's well – I like him, and Oscar's murder was horrible," she added. With this the interview ended, and Susan left the police station, nodding and saying good-bye to Parker.

(4) Oscar's Black Book

With Parker by his side, Detective Brendan rang the Murray's front door. They were following up on the Sergeant's request to check the Murray' furnace. Ruthy answered, "Good afternoon, Detective Brendan. What brings you back here and who's your friend?"

"Good afternoon, Mrs. Murray. This is Mr. Spooner, a private investigator, who helps the police. We were wondering if we could check out your furnace?"

"Come in and I'll take you to the basement." The men followed her to the downstairs steps as she talked, "With warmer weather, we haven't used the new gas furnace much since we got it, but it's been working well."

"That's for certain," said her husband, John, who joined the group as they went down into the basement. "It's really good to have finally converted to gas heat, especially now that I'm getting older. I don't have to worry about coal deliveries anymore."

"We should have converted to gas heat years ago," added Ruthy, "we're one of the last to make the switch from coal to gas, but it finally happened for us at the end of April."

Standing before the new gas furnace, Parker and Brendan merely looked at each other wistfully.
The prior black book had been thrown into the coal furnace, which had now been replaced.

"When workers came to replace the old coal furnace and to install the new gas furnace do you know if they happened to find a black book?" inquired Parker.

"Why yes," said a surprised Ruthy, "they gave me a black book. It had a lot of numbers and initials of names in it, and none of it made much sense to me. I have it upstairs in a drawer and can get it for you if you want." Parker had a big smile as he nodded yes, and Ruthy went upstairs and returned holding Oscar's black book.

"Thank you," said Parker as he opened the book. The first line read: 10/12 2nd Sam P. $5 Top Class 1st L followed by a second line 10/12 4th Trixie $2 Play Good Twice 1st L followed by 10/12 4th Phil K. $10 Big Brown 1st L followed by 10/12 5th Amos C. $10 Lite Up Lou 1st W (pay $15.20).

"It's horse racing results from last October 12th," said Detective Brendan, looking over Parker's shoulder.

"Yes," said Parker, "and it's clear that the first three bettors lost $5, $2, and $10 for a total of $17 into Oscar's pocket and then the fourth bet for $10 was a winner and received $15.20 meaning that last bet cost Oscar $5.20."

"The book just goes on and on and look at the second page; that's World Series game 3 from October 12, 1971, where Pittsburgh defeated Baltimore," said Detective Brendan.

"Yes, there's a lot of information here, and it will take me hours to go through the entire book," observed Parker scrolling through its pages.

"What will you be looking for?"

"I'll have to think about it, but probably large bets, frequent bettors, and perhaps names of folks like the Glueck brothers, who have a reputation of dishonesty."

“Man, Parker,” said Detective Brendan, “I don’t envy you going through all that data, but I guess part of your actuarial training was to look at lots of detailed numbers and make sense of them.”

“Yes, the first five examinations to become a life insurance actuary require mathematical skills and the ability to sort through reams of data, sorting out relevant facts from those that aren’t.”

Looking over their shoulders at what was written in the black book was John Murray who asked,
“Who’s Top Class, Trixie, and Play Good Twice?”

“If you look at the order of the names, you will see that Top Class and Play Good Twice are the names of the horses being bet on, while Trixie is a person who bet $2 on Play Good Twice and lost that bet - that’s the letter L.” explained Parker.

“Oh, yeah, that’s clear now,” said John, “and I see some guy Phil K. lost $10 on Big Bunny, while Amos C. won playing Lite Up Lou. So this is what Oscar did to make money.”

“That’s it John. Now remember, this is the black book Oscar threw away to be burned. He was using a new black book that’s missing. That book may have the name of his killer so if it should somehow turn up, you’ll let Detective Brendan know. Okay?”

“Okay,” replied a beaming John Murray, having understood for the first time Oscar’s bets in the notorious black book that his deceased tenant carried everywhere.

As Parker was leaving the basement, he noticed a stack of books in the corner and the one on top was titled "Life Contingencies" by C.W. Jordan. It had a bright red cover and was known as Red Jordan to actuaries in order to distinguish it from the prior version that had a blue cover. If you mastered Red Jordan, you were on your way to becoming a life insurance actuary. "That's an important book for a future actuary, and it's a surprise for me to see it here," remarked Parker looking at Ruthy.

"That entire stack of books belongs to John's nephew, Edward, who was cleaning out his apartment months ago and somehow they wound up in our basement," said Ruthy.

"Is your nephew, Edward, an actuary, Mr. Murray?" asked Parker as he continued to look at the papers and books stacked up in the corner.

"No, he's not an actuary but a few years ago he was thinking about it. He got his physics degree from the University of Chicago and wound up working at Argonne National Laboratory. He lives out there and comes often into the city on weekends. We gave Edward our house key, and he has a cot upstairs in our small bedroom that he uses, and we're always happy to see him," replied John.

At that moment, Parker noticed a stack of papers labeled Argonne National Laboratory. He thought that they deserved additional scrutiny, so he folded them to review later and placed them in his pocket.

Parker also noted Ruthy's remark that Edward had a key to the house, which meant an entrance to Oscar's upstairs apartment. Additionally, the mortality table on the back of the note asking for money almost certainly came from the basement corner where Red Jordan and other material resided. Thus, Edward, with a key to the house, had access to both the second floor where Oscar lived and to the basement where the actuarial and other material were located. Parker would keep that in mind as he proceeded with his investigation of Oscar's murder. With that, Detective Brendan and Parker excused themselves and left Murray's house.

Later that evening after the kids had gone to bed, Rosemary was taking her shower, and Parker began looking at the Argonne papers that he had folded earlier. They were notes that Edward had taken at work. The first page had lots of scribbles and drawings on it and the words 'start developing an electronic translator of animal sounds.' The last six words were underlined. That was followed by several pages of scribbles and a detailed drawing of a device that looked like the electronic translator mentioned earlier. Occasionally, a word such as 'frequency' was clear, but most of the words were abbreviated or identified by initials. The last page had top secret written on it followed by the words work starts next week, team effort, no future notes allowed. These pages were clearly part of the meeting that announced the start of the top-secret project that Edward would be working on with others.

Parker also had Oscar's black book. He put Edward's notes down and began turning the pages of Oscar's black book that Ruthy had given him. Almost immediately he spotted a monthly recurring entry: FJ $2,500. Oscar was receiving $2,500 every month from FJ and that didn't seem to be any sort of bet, but a payment for some service that Oscar was rendering to whoever FJ was. The $2,500 was far greater than any of the bets being placed by Oscar's regular customers. Nothing else was immediately noteworthy, and Parker put the black book on his night table a few minutes after Rosemary came out of the bathroom. She quickly climbed into bed and started saying her evening prayers. When completed, Rosemary smiled at Parker saying in her usual joking manner, "Should I be concerned that my darling husband now has a black book of names?"

"No concern, my love, for this black book only indicates that your darling husband has now embarked on another case for the father of his lovely wife."

"Oh no, what does my father have you involved with now?"

"A rather gruesome murder – no suspects thus far – and also no insights."

"Sounds like another exciting murder case, my darling husband, to divert your attention away from the staid actuary certifying boring reserves for insurers" said Rosemary, kissing her husband good night. Parker smiled at this, noticing that his murder case was 'exciting' to Rosemary while the actuary was a 'staid' person and certified 'boring reserves'.

The next day was Sunday, June 4, 1972, and the entire Parker family went to Sunday mass. The family lived in Hyde Park, a section of Chicago where the University of Chicago was located, and their eldest child, John, was completing his freshman year at the college. He had elected to live at home rather than residing in a school dormitory. The same was going to be true for Grace who was graduating from high school and would be attending the University as a freshman in September. Thus, the entire family would continue to be together on Sundays for mass, and so it was on this Sunday.

The mass celebration was for the second Sunday after Pentecost and the gospel reading was Luke Ch. 14 v. 16-24 where a man made a great supper and many of the invited made excuses not to attend, and thus the tables were subsequently filled with the poor, feeble, blind, lame, and those from the highways and hedges.

Father Joseph was the mass celebrant, and he read from the new American Bible printed by the Catholic Book Publishing Company: "Jesus responded: "A man was giving a large dinner and he invited many. At dinner time he sent his servant to say to those invited, 'Come along, everything is ready now,' But they began to excuse themselves, one and all. The first one said to the servant, 'I have bought some land and must go out and inspect it. Please excuse me.' Another said, 'I have bought five yokes of oxen, and I am going out to test them. Please excuse me.' A third said, 'I am newly married and so I cannot come.' The servant returning reported all of this to his master. The master of the house grew angry at the account. He said to his servant, 'Go out quickly into the streets and alleys of the town and bring in the poor and the crippled, the blind and the lame.' The servant reported, after some time, 'Your orders have been carried out, my lord, and there is still room.' The master then said to the servant, 'Go out into the highways and along the hedgerows and force them to come in. I want my house to be full, but I tell you that not one of those invited shall taste a morsel of my dinner.''""

Parker and his family reflected on the gospel words and the fact that many folks didn't attend Sunday morning mass because they had other priorities. Yet the invitation to participate in mass was there, and its celebration was open to everyone.

After church, the Spooner family went for Pizza at Medici, followed by a walk around the UC campus, making it home to read the Sunday papers while the kids hit their school books for their final tests. According to the Chicago Tribune, the police were releasing Oscar's body to a funeral home. Oscar did not have a family, but an executor of his estate had come forward, and the burial would be on Tuesday at Woodlawn Cemetery in Forest Park, Illinois. The closed casket service for Oscar would be that morning at the funeral home. Parker decided he would attend.

(5) Crime Scene Results

Sergeant Boyle set up an early Monday morning meeting to discuss the laboratory results of the crime scene where Oscar was murdered and to update his staff regarding the prior police investigation of the Glueck brothers. Besides Detective Brendan, another detective and two uniform policemen were in attendance along with a stenographer.

The Sergeant had the results of Oscar's murder investigation on a pad of paper, and he relayed what he was reading. "Oscar was blood type 0+. He bled profusely, and his blood was all over the floor. Somehow, there also was a small amount of blood type AB- on the counter. The killer must have cut himself. AB- is a very rare blood type and may be helpful down the road identifying the killer. The knife that killed him had a long blade. That suggests that killer may have had it hidden when he entered the apartment. Perhaps he carried it in a large bag or had it hidden under his jacket if he wore one. The knife markings on the victim's throat were also consistent with a switchblade that snaps open and has a long knife blade."

Here, Sergeant Boyle paused and turned the page; continuing, "There were fingerprints in the apartment. Besides Oscar's prints, there was a very good set close to the kitchen sink on the counter and away from the table where the murder occurred. These prints match a set of prints on file here. They belong to a woman, Susan Danford, who we questioned last Saturday about the murder. She denied being in the apartment recently, but this set was fresh, so Susan had knowing lied to us. We'll have to bring her back in and confront her regarding her lie. Oscar and Susan dated for four months of this year and then separated because she wanted marriage and Oscar didn't. We don't believe Susan could have done the murder because she's not tall enough to have gotten behind Oscar and cut downward across his throat. Assuming Susan isn't the killer, then Oscar's killer did not leave any prints."

The Sergeant picked up another file indicating that the Glueck brothers were already being investigated and that he had started receiving reports discussing them. He read, "When Linda Glueck died, her two sons didn't know what they were going to do. They found their way by joining various street gangs and soon learned about jewelry and how to make money by selling fake diamonds and emeralds and other imitation stones. They kept fairly much to themselves, trusting no one and keeping associates and women at a distance without removing them completely from the daily routine. The brothers also were known to come down quickly on anyone who crossed them, but they have never been charged with a major crime."

The Sergeant paused, "I also have a report from a police operative who was watching the brothers and saw them pass a small package to Oscar Busby in Grant Park on Memorial Day, just a few days ago. The three men talked briefly but nothing else was exchanged. After the brothers walked away, the operative reported that Oscar wrote in his black book."

Here the Sergeant speculated that the brothers had placed a bet with Oscar and paid him with some of their jewelry, which was in the small package that Oscar received. Perhaps the Glueck brothers had won their bet, were looking for their money, and came to Oscar's apartment to collect. Things got out of hand and the brothers killed Oscar.

Boyle then quickly added that what he had just said didn't make much sense. Why would Oscar accept a jewelry bet if he and Susan had separated? Had Oscar found another girl friend? Didn't Oscar know or suspect that the Glueck brothers dealt in fake jewelry? If he knew about the fake jewelry, perhaps he didn't care. Also, the Sergeant wondered what happened to the jewelry that Oscar had recently received based on the report of the police operative. Did Oscar return it? Or did the murderer(s) take it along with the black book after the murder?

Sergeant Boyle said he was also surprised that a police operative was watching the brothers. Clearly someone in the chain of command had placed them under surveillance, yet the Sergeant hadn't been informed. He said he would have to find out what was happening. Why were the brothers being watched and what were they doing the night Oscar was murdered? The Sergeant was upset that he did not know about the surveillance, yet the brothers lived in his police district. He wondered if his boss, Lieutenant Gary Cambe, knew and had not notified the Sergeant. The Sergeant would then be annoyed at Cambe, which was the normal state of affairs.

(6) Miami's CIA Office

Special agent Frank Jenkins, who ran the Miami Central Intelligence Agency or CIA office, was now looking at the city of Chicago and the murder of Oscar Busby since that murder would impact his office's local work. Oscar had been one of his agents in the Chicago area. The CIA was a civilian foreign intelligence agency of the federal government. They were tasked with advancing national security through collecting and studying intelligence from around the world, and they conducted covert operations. However, before Frank got too involved with the Busby murder, Jenkins had to deal with the scheduled meeting of his three teams.

Team A was headed by agent Stein, who was punctual and organized, looking at his notebook, and now pacing in an outer office as he usually did to keep his weight down while waiting for his counterparts. Team B was headed by agent Watts, who had been born in England and came to the United States as a teenager with his parents shortly after World War II ended. He was teased for using expressions such as "Blimey" and was seated in Jenkins' office reading a newspaper looking for soccer news, which he called football news, but soccer news was difficult to find in American sports pages even during the regular season which ran in Europe from late August into May. Of course, it was now June, yet Watts was still hopeful to see final team standings and updates. Agent Williams, who headed Team C, was missing and now late, as usual. Jenkins slammed the classified report that he had been reading onto his desk and rang the intraoffice buzzer with a truculence not entirely foreign to his nature. An agile and pert blonde secretary wearing the latest pants-suit outfit glided into the office, "Yes, sir, you rang?"

"Miss Qundo, tell agent Williams to get up here on the double for our meeting!" growled Jenkins.

"On the double, yes sir." She quickly left the room. Miss Aurelia Qundo noticed that Jenkins' desk was once again a mess of papers. Every morning before he came into his office, she would straighten out his desk so that it would be easy for him to find his folders and papers. He was appreciative of this, but otherwise he was completely focused on the work of the Agency, and Miss Qundo was disappointed that he didn't pay attention to her as a woman, or if he did, then he was being very coy about it. That was her hope because even though Frank Jenkins was fifteen years older than her, she was falling in love with him. Moreover, she was saddened to see despite her best efforts, that by midday his desk was back to a complete mess. Moreover, she really wasn't a secretary – that was her cover as established by Jenkins - but had been hired because of her high intelligence and college degrees in marine biology. In fact, Aurelia Qundo was involved in a secret classified CIA project where she was still learning, and only Frank Jenkins knew all the details.

Waiting for Williams, Jenkins stood at the office window and watched the jets land at the nearby Miami airport. Long strings of gray, oily-looking smoke trailed each plane and hung for several seconds in the sky before dissipating into the general haze. Invariably, he lit a cigarette, and then with a curse quickly extinguished it. Ever since the Surgeon General's 1964 report that cigarettes were harmful and caused cancer, he vowed to break his smoking habit, but eight years later he had not yet stopped the habit of lighting and extinguishing a cigarette when he was deep in thought about a national security problem. Although he was focused on his work, he knew that he was attracted to the looks and brains of Aurelia or Miss Qundo as he called her, but he would never show that in an outward manner.

His current reverie was broken when agent Williams bounded into the office. "Miss Qundo said the meeting was starting."

"Sit down," growled Jenkins to Williams. Agents Stein and Watts were already seated in Jenkins' office, and as Williams sat, Miss Qundo left the room, closing the door behind her

"The purpose of this meeting is to announce that I've hired a new agent who will initially lead a new small team. For the time being Agent D will remain anonymous. His territory will be the Atlantic Ocean - I stress the Ocean - from Key West north to Cape Kennedy so initially there should be no interference with any of your projects. If boats or ships are coming in or leaving the docks – those docks are land and that is still your territory, but what's under the docks in many places is water and Team D will worry about what's happening there, the Atlantic Ocean itself, and everything under the sea. I've asked Miss Qundo to coordinate our new fourth team or Team D into our work, so you'll be contacting her if anything develops in your work that impacts ocean activities, and she will notify you if agent D finds anything that may impact your team. Are there any initial questions about this development?"

The three men looked at each other. There had been indications that something was happening internally within the CIA along the Miami - Fort Lauderdale docks and specifically there were two individuals, Boris Volkov and Dmitry Doby, that had been identified as likely spies for the Soviet Union, and thus they were under surveillance by the three teams. In particular, Boris Volkov was gathering information with frequent boat excursions out into the ocean along the south Florida coast. Apparently, it was serious enough now that a new agent D and a team D were formed to handle the situation that was happening in the ocean.

Williams raised his hand, "The recent reports that I've been filing about the docks in my territory will impact team D because our surveillance of Boris Volkov indicates that he's likely meeting with someone out on the ocean and then passing that information to Dmitry Doby who works out of a Miami house. We aren't certain what Dmitry does with this information."

"Yes," answered Jenkins, "and the Agency cannot allow this to continue indefinitely. We have to be in a position to arrest these men before the situation gets out of control. I will ask Miss Qundo to help you, agent Williams, with warrants for their arrest and to start the paper work to present our case to the judges. I think we'll have to move against them soon, likely before the end of this summer, and I want to start the paperwork now so that we're not rushed in September."

Agent Williams became excited because he took delight at every opportunity to work with Miss Qundo. She was young, only in her twenties, and drop-dead gorgeous. Only five years out of a prestigious southern university studying marine biology, she had been active in the civil rights movement during the mid-60's and had been raised in various locations as her father was a Navy captain. Williams touched his mustache again as he had a habit of doing. He knew the Florida agency did not permit dating other people who worked for the agency. Yet Aurelia - thinking of Miss Qundo by her first name – yes, Aurelia was a very beautiful woman with that long golden hair and besides her physical beauty she was also very bright. In every way, a perfect woman thought agent Williams.

While agent Williams fantasized about Miss Qundo, Special Agent Frank Jenkins sat back in his chair and went into a long think about what he was going to do. He looked out his window at the jet planes landing at the Miami airport. When he started at the CIA as a young man, nearly twenty years ago, there were only propeller planes flying for civilians, but now it was jet planes. The world was moving rapidly. Meanwhile, agents Stein and Watts looked at each other. Jenkins had just announced a new agent, agent D, who would remain anonymous. They expected more details, but apparently that wasn't going to happen because Jenkins was now concentrating on two potential spies, namely Boris Volkov and Dmitry Doby, and arresting them within months.

Jenkins confirmed that when he suddenly turned around and excused agents Stein and Watts, "Thank you, we'll talk more about agent D as time passes," and then after they exited he said to agent Williams, "Ask Miss Qundo to come in here so I can inform her about the arrest warrants that the two of you will prepare for the upcoming arrests of Boris Volkov and Dmitry Doby." With this news, Agent Williams heart leaped – he and Aurelia would finally be working together on a case!

Agent Williams could hardly suppress his excitement as he approached Miss Qundo with the news. She remained impassive as the two walked back into Jenkins' office to receive their instructions. It turned out that Jenkins had them working separately, each in their own offices. Miss Qundo would gather information from Dmitry's file which was on her desk, while Williams would work from Boris's file which was on his desk.

Additionally, after Miss Qundo left Jenkins' office, Jenkins asked Williams to stay. He then told Williams about Oscar's murder. This was a big problem for the Agency because Oscar's death was almost certainly related to his recent discovery of a Soviet spy that he was about to reveal. Jenkins then gave Williams an additional assignment. Agent Williams cursed his bad luck. He and Aurelia working on arrest warrants would not bring them together as Williams had initially supposed. Not only were they preparing arrest warrants for different individuals, but now Williams had a new and separate assignment that would take him out of the office. Agent Williams returned to his desk pouting about this assignment and his misfortune of having Aurelia working separately on information for Dmitry Doby while he had to handle Boris Volkov's file.

This separation from working directly with Aurelia was bothering him to such an extent that when Miss Qundo was ready to leave the office for the evening, Agent Williams could not contain himself any longer and decided to act. He approached her, "Allow me to walk you to your car."

She did not respond, and they both entered the elevator, which had other people in it. They rode it down to the first floor, crossed the lobby and walked out together into the parking lot. Miss Qundo stopped in front of a white Mercedes. "This is my car," she said.

"Given the importance of our actions in preparing these arrest warrants, I wonder if I might see you later tonight?" asked Agent Williams, nervously fingering his mustache as he was close to officially breaking the Agency's code of conduct even though he had carefully not directly asked her out for dinner or a drink. Her reply was made unintelligible by a jet that roared overhead approaching its landing at the airport. Miss Qundo tightly clasped her ears with her hands and closed her eyes. The entire earth shook as Williams struggled to understand what she had just answered. "Excuse me?" he said when the noise of the jet finally subsided.

"I'm busy tonight," replied Miss Qundo sweetly. She strapped her alligator purse across her shoulder and quickly drove away. Disappointed, Williams watched her car maneuver for space against heavy traffic on the overcrowded ramp leading to the expressway. He wondered how a secretary could afford a Mercedes and, in that moment, recognized that her role in the Agency was much higher than the duties of a secretary.

With that, his early joy of working with Aurelia turned to sorrow as another low flying jet roared overhead, and Agent Williams knew that he was not going to get close to Miss Qundo. This disturbed Williams as did the announcement of a new unidentified agent. "Who is agent D and why don't we know his name?" muttered Williams to himself followed by "I wonder if Miss Qundo knows his name?"

(7) Developments

It was Monday morning when Parker opened his office door, snapped on the light, placed his briefcase on the desk, and turned on the window air conditioner. Looking out his window over the air conditioner, Parker could see a portion of Chicago's Museum of Science and Industry. Walking back to his desk, he transferred his briefcase from the desk to the floor and slightly loosened his tie. Parker always wore a suit and tie in his office. There were two photographs on his desk and two paintings on the wall behind his desk. The first photo showed a young Parker and his bride, Rosmary Boyle, on their wedding day. The second photo was recent and showed the entire family with John who was finishing his first year of college, Grace who was in her last year of high school, Peter who was in sixth grade, and Anna who was in kindergarten. Behind Parker's desk were two paintings: one of George Washington taking the oath of office as President of the United States of America, and the other of Jesus as the Good Shepherd.

Parker opened his briefcase and removed Oscar's black book. He was looking for bets made by David G. or Donald G., the two Glueck's brothers, and there were very few and none for a significant amount of money. Moreover, the black book, if it contained any secrets to the murder of Oscar Busby at all, was not going to reveal anything quickly. Who was FJ and why was FJ giving Oscar $2,500 every month? That was $30,000 in one year and serious money in 1970 when the average salary was more like $10,000. To Parker that seemed to be the only question that immediately came to mind after looking at multiple entries recorded in Oscar's black book. At that moment, the telephone rang, "Good morning, son-in-law. If you have time, I would like to update you on Oscar's murder," said Sergeant Boyle on the other end.

"Go ahead, Dad, I've time to listen."

"Regarding the Glueck Brothers, I found out that Lieutenant Cambe had put them under surveillance several weeks ago because of a tip that they were about to receive some fake diamonds." Parker knew that Lieutenant Gary Cambe was Michael Boyle's immediate boss in the Chicago Police Department's chain of command. Cambe was not well liked, being a taciturn individual by nature, and the Sergeant and detectives were happy he worked in a different office in downtown Chicago. In this matter Lieutenant Cambe had not conveyed the surveillance of the Glueck brothers to all his sergeants, and Sergeant Boyle only found about it because he requested an informational search of Cambe's police files. "Anyway," continued Sergeant Boyle, "no fake diamond shipment has yet arrived at their jewelry store, however, in early April Oscar was observed buying earrings from them."

"That ties in with Susan's story that she received earrings from Oscar," said Parker.

"Yes, but he also bought some jewelry from them over the Memorial Day weekend; and of more importance, surveillance revealed that the Glueck brothers were in their jewelry store the entire day of the murder. However, in the evening they went to a pub to eat and drink, and then they somehow ditched surveillance around 10:30 pm. At that point they may have gone home or to Oscar's place or somewhere else. We know they returned to their store on Thursday morning. In short, they could have committed the murder, but we don't know where or what they were doing at eleven o'clock that Wednesday evening. We're going to pay them a visit today to get their version of where they were last Wednesday night. The exchange of jewelry over

Memorial Day indicates that they had a bet with Oscar. Perhaps they went to collect it that night. LOOK TO COLLECT ALL MONEY BY ELEVEN was the note Oscar had when his body was discovered. Perhaps Oscar didn't have the money when the collectors arrived, and they killed him."

The Sergeant paused, and Parker said, "The mortality table on the opposite side of the note suggests that it was written on paper that came from the Murrays basement. The only folks who have access to that basement are John, Ruthy, Edward, and Oscar himself who lived upstairs."

"Exactly," replied the Sergeant, "We're going to talk to the three Murrays this Wednesday afternoon – John at 1 pm, Ruthy at 2, and Edward at 3. If you would like to join us in the side room to view the interviews, let me know."

"Yes, I'll be there," replied Parker.

"Now with respect to Susan Danford," continued the Sergeant, "her fresh fingerprints are in Oscar's kitchen, so she deliberately lied to me when she claimed that she hadn't been in his apartment recently. We'll get Miss Danford back here shortly to find out the reason for her lie. It really doesn't make sense to me. She didn't have to allow us to fingerprint her. She said she had nothing to hide and wasn't in Oscar's apartment the night of the murder or even recently. Yet her fingerprints were found in his apartment and show she was lying." Boyle shook his head sadly.

"I wonder why she was in his apartment that night?" said Parker. "Did Susan and Oscar really split up as Susan claimed and was this meeting an attempt to get back together? If she walked out that night and Oscar was still alive, then the killer arrived shortly thereafter. They must have just missed each other."

"Exactly right," answered Sergeant Boyle, "perhaps Susan and Oscar didn't split up but then why the ruse? And the timing of her late-night visit to him so close to the murder is another puzzle, assuming that she *didn't* kill him, which is highly likely given that someone tall grabbed him from the rear and cut his throat."

"The fact that the Glueck brothers managed to lose their surveillance the night of the murder may indicate that they knew they were being watched. What else do we know about these brothers?"

"Very little, other than they run a jewelry store and are suspected of selling fake jewelry."

There's no known connection between the brothers and Susan Danford?"

The Sergeant said, "That's correct and also there's no known connection between the brothers and Bob Hanson, who packed his bags and left for somewhere unknown early Friday morning according to his landlady. That's not normal behavior for Bob Hanson"

"You're correct, Dad, none of this makes any sense right now, but we've only just started our investigation. It's still early, and we've got to learn more about Oscar and who he was."

(8) Lt. Gary Cambe

Lieutenant Gary Cambe, Seargeant Michael Boyle's boss in the Chicago police hierarchy, went after the Glueck brothers in March 1972 by having them tailed every day. They were small time crooks, and the Lieutenant was looking for an ex-con, who went by the handle, Mic the Knife. He thought he could find Mic the Knife through the Glueck brothers since the brothers had grown up with Mic.

During one of the days when the brothers purchased fake diamonds from their Florida source, Cambe's operative saw the transaction and within an hour the Glueck brothers were hauled into the downtown police station where the Lieutenant resided. Immediately, the Lieutenant was on the job and started questioning them. Gary Cambe was big, bulky, and stood tall at 6 feet, 3 inches with lots of black hair, blue eyes, and a round jaw.

"You're telling me these diamonds are fake – if so, my brother and I didn't know this," said David Glueck, sitting up very straight and puffing his muscular chest and arms forward. "We've done nothing wrong," added Donald Glueck softly, "I think we have to be silent and call for a lawyer."

"I'm not arresting you, right now," snapped Lieutenant Cambe, "but perhaps you could help me and the Chicago police on another matter."

With that, the two brothers looked at each other and then nodded to the Lieutenant to continue. They knew that the Lieutenant was knowledgeable about the neighborhoods he policed.

"There's a local guy that David went to school with and who is probably also known to Donald. On the street, this man is called Mic the Knife," said the Lieutenant.

"Yea," said David, "that would be Michael Klossmeier. He's one tough dude, and I went to high school with him."

"I know Mike also," said Donald.

"Yes, that's him, Michael Klossmeier. I would like to talk to him – face to face – if I knew where he lived. Is that something you could do for me?" asked Cambe.

"You want us to arrange a meeting for you with Mike Klossmeier?" asked David incredulously.

"Yes, I'm not interested in arresting him, but I want to have a friendly talk with him," replied a smiling Lieutenant Cambe. "Do you know where he is?"

"No, I haven't seen him in months," said David, "I thought he was in jail."

"Me, neither" replied Donald, "but I heard he had been released from prison even though I haven't seen him."

"He was in prison for stabbing a person during a fight. Some people say he's murdered others with his knife, but he's never been arrested for murder. Records show he was released six months ago, having served his time for that stabbing. He's no longer at the address or phone number given when he reentered society. I hope to find him. Once again, this has nothing to do with arresting him. He's served his time, and there's no evidence that he murdered anyone or did anything else wrong. I simply would like to talk to him. Any ideas about where he might be?"

The two brothers looked at one another. Donald said, "It's a long shot but I heard that he may be renting an apartment in the house of a mother whose daughter Marsha I know from high school."

"That may be a very good lead," said Lieutenant Cambe, "If you guys could go to work on this and locate Mike or Mic for me, that would be great. Here's my card, one for each of you, with my phone number. Once you locate him, his address in particular, get back to me with that information, and I'll take it from there. Don't mention to him that I'm a cop; that would just make him nervous, and he might run away. I assure you that I'm not out to arrest him. I just have to talk to this guy, which I will once you give me his current address." With that, the Lieutenant sat back in his chair and smiled before concluding, "We're confiscating these fake diamonds, and don't do it again because next time I won't say as I'm saying now that the two of you are free to go. I'm doing you a favor by allowing you to go because you haven't sold these fake diamonds and you're doing me a favor by locating Mic."

Outside the police station in downtown Chicago, the Glueck brothers looked at each other completely surprised at what had just happened. Donald said to his brother, "I'm fairly certain I know where Mic the Knife has been living. I'll just check it out and get the address from Marsha. Then I'll call the Lieutenant with that info."

"Yea, that should be easy, but we just lost our fake diamonds and probably can't get more of them given that the cops are watching us," replied David.

"Yea, but now what are we going to do for money? How are we going to live?" asked Donald.

"Now that we know we're being watched, we'll have to devise a plan to work around their surveillance. We certainly can't leave a profitable business," replied David.

Donald smiled at his older brother and became confident that they would be back in business very soon. A stiff Chicago wind made this day in the month of March uncomfortably cold, forcing the Glueck brothers into a warm pub.

Neither one of the brothers, although surprised that their fake diamonds had been discovered by the police, wondered why Lieutenant Cambe went to them rather than his own police force to find out where Mic was currently living.

(9) Mic, Marsha, and Delia

Michael Klossmeier also known as Mic the Knife, was now living as a tenant in the basement of a rundown house on the south side of Chicago near the now nearly defunct Stock Yards. The house was owned by Mrs. Delia Dempsey who was 45 years old and worked as a waitress at a nearby restaurant. She had married young and a year later Marsha was born. This proved too much for the father who deserted his family when the baby was a year old. Marsha who was now twenty-one also lived in the house and was a waitress on a different shift at the same restaurant. Marsha had an inquisitive mind and also went to night school at a junior college obtaining credits with the idea of obtaining a full college degree in some particular area to be determined soon. She had the reputation of being unconventional and a bit of a risk taker. Mic was not related to the Dempsey's and had been recently released from jail for a stabbing he committed. Almost immediately after his release, he went to a dentist and had a missing tooth replaced. He looked in a mirror and was very pleased with what he saw. He was back to his former handsome self. He started dating Marsha, who was a good-looking young woman, and soon Mic was their basement tenant.

Mic told Marsha that he would have a big job and lots of money and then would buy a house for himself in Madison, Wisconsin. He said Marsha was free to join him living there. Marsha believed him and that's when she talked her skeptical mother into the temporary basement arrangement for Mic. Delia wasn't happy with this arrangement but the possibility of her quick-witted but impulsive daughter living with Mic on the street was far worse. Delia was also worried about her own health. Having a man around the house paying rent money for the basement and perhaps helping with a chore or two made sense to her.

Time passed quickly, and Mic came into possession of a green 1952 Studebaker with its identifying bullet front. He was a little nervous fixing it because he knew it wouldn't last long on the street. But by then he had joined a group of neighborhood guys and collectively they helped each other. There was Skip who worked as a mechanic at a nearby garage. He was always taking apart old cars and putting them back together. There was Bruno, a happy-go-lucky husky fellow who specialized in fixing up or repairing apartments and houses. Bruno not only painted the walls and ceilings, but he could construct cabinets and chairs to spruce up the interior. Big Steve worked at one of the local banks and was helpful with financial advice. He also was good for a low-cost loan that he financed himself for a short period of time. These guys palled around with Mic, and the group went several times to Comiskey Park to watch the Chicago White Sox play baseball. In 1972, it was the oldest ballpark in the major leagues and had a very deep center field and an exploding score board. The Chicago White Sox were also doing well that year, which attracted many fans to the ballpark, and they wound up with a winning record finishing second to the Oakland Athletics who won the American League West, and then the American League Champion Series, and finally the World Series.

That spring, Skip helped Mic get the Studebaker engine running well, while Mic, in turn, helped clean up and organize Skip's garage which was a mess. Bruno cleaned the white interior of the car while Mic helped organize Bruno's multiple tool kits. It was Big Steve who suggested Mic check out the affordable houses available in Madison Wisconsin. By the end of May, the Studebaker was operating well and road tested. Mic and his friends kept watch on it at night. Mic told his friends that he would soon be driving the car up to Wisconsin to buy a house, and then he would invite everyone to come over for a big party.

Delia was watching all of this from afar. She was pleased that Mic now had a car but was apprehensive about his apparent new-found money. It was clear but strange to her that somehow, he now possessed a large sum of money and could afford to buy a house in Madison. Marsha told her mother that Mic would be moving up there, and she would be visiting him on some weekends to see what was happening. Delia's common sense told her that if Mic had suddenly come into serious money, then it was almost certain he was up to no good. She was worried for her daughter either way – if he came into illegal money and Marsha went with him to Wisconsin, then there would be heartbreak for her daughter when he was caught. On the other hand, if Mic played her for a foolish woman and ran out on her, then Marsha would be heartbroken at being dumped. There was nothing Delia could do but wait and see what transpired since her daughter was erratically bright but generally did not listen to her mother. At the same time, Marsha could and did change her mind very quickly, which was a practical reason for Delia to remain calm. If something went wrong, she knew her daughter was smart enough to figure out the problem and correct it.

It would be unknown to Delia, but Marsha would soon come to the attention of the Chicago police, and once Lieutenant Gary Cambe learned that Marsha and Mic might be an item, the Lieutenant wanted to talk to Marsha in his office.

(10) Oscar's Funeral

On the day of Oscar's burial, the funeral home was packed with people and most of them were men who played chess. They came to pay their respect to a man who loved to play 5-minute chess, a struggle where each player had 5 minutes to make all his moves or lose the game on time. Many players could get a winning position but could not find the winning line or idea and would then lose the game when their flag fell on the clock because they had used up their five minutes. This was the way Oscar won many "theoretically lost" positions and collected the agreed to bet. He was a master when it came to winning in this manner, and many players returned to play him again and again because they had a winning position before and were certain they could beat him the next time they played. This happened enough for Oscar to always have extra money in his pocket and to carry a chess clock, board, and pieces wherever he traveled, looking for the next "fish" for him to fry.

Parker was at the funeral for the burial and recognized most of the chess players. Certainly, all the players he and the Sergeant had interviewed at the Gompers Park Chess Club were present including Barry Snyder, Frank Costello, Pavel Kotov, Jackson, Lev, and Kyle, along with Susan Danford, however, Bob Hanson remained among the missing.

As Parker circulated through the crowd, he spotted a tall middle-aged man with a mustache that he didn't recognize. This person was dressed in a good-looking dark blue suit, which was not unusual for a funeral, even though many of the chess players only wore sport jackets without ties. Curious about the stranger, Parker asked Barry who the man with the mustache was, and Barry said he had never seen him.

Parker then approached John and Ruthy Murray standing next to another tall man who wore a light brown suit. This person was young, clean shaven, and sported a crew cut. "Parker Spooner, let me introduce you to my nephew, Edward Murray, who works at the Argonne National Laboratory," said John. "Edward, Mr. Spooner is a private investigator and helps the police with their investigations."

"Very glad to meet you, sir," said the young man, shaking Parker's hand.

"Nice to meet you, Edward. Having graduated from the University of Chicago in the late 1940s, I'm familiar with the Argonne National Laboratory," remarked Parker.

Realizing that mustache man was closely watching them, Parker shifted his position slightly turning the back of his head on the observing intruder and blocking Edward's face so that the observer could no longer read their lips.

"Oh, yes," replied Edward, "everyone who works at Argonne knows the University of Chicago because Argonne was born out of the University's work on the Manhattan Project in the 1940s which developed the atomic bomb and gave the world nuclear energy."

"Yes, Stagg field is gone, replaced by a monument to nuclear fission," answered Parker.

"I don't care about the sculpture that was erected there. It looks like a human skull or a mushroom cloud," said Edward.

"The wording at the site does commemorate that Enrico Fermi and his team achieved the first controlled self-sustaining nuclear chain reaction on December 2, 1942, initiating the atomic age," replied Parker. "They wanted to document that the event happened at the University of Chicago under the stands of a football field."

"Yes, but Argonne National Laboratory now develops peaceful uses of nuclear energy. Fermi's experiment showed nuclear fission was possible, and it led to the atomic bomb, which is well in the past. I'm happy to be working at Argonne on the many peaceful uses of nuclear energy," emphasized Edward.

"Edward, I would like to talk to you more. Perhaps we could meet for lunch one of these days," said Parker.

"Here's my card and phone number at work. You can join me at lunch at Argonne, but you're going to have to pass a security check first. Let me know when you're ready." Parker took Edward's card and noted that the young Murray had a master's degree in physics.

At that moment a nondenominational Christian minister from a nearby church asked everyone to take a seat so that he could say a few words in memory of Oscar. Edward, John, and Ruthy took seats in the front row while Parker moved to the rear as the minister directed people with his hands before beginning his sermon.

"Friends, we are gathered here to say farewell to our friend and fellow chess player, Oscar Busby. Oscar was an amazing man – always up for a chess game and a man who was very knowledgeable about all sporting events. His tragic death may give us all a pause, but we can take consolation in the words of scripture. I turn in particular to Mark 4, verses 35-41, which describes a sudden storm on the sea."

The minister opened his bible and started to read: “That day as evening drew on, he said to them. Let us cross over to the farther shore. Leaving the crowd, they took him away in the boat in which he was sitting, while the other boats accompanied him. It happened that a bad squall blew up. The waves were breaking over the boat, and it began to ship water badly.”

He paused, “Yes, friends, as this passage indicates, something bad may suddenly happen.”

The minister then continued reading, “Jesus was in the stern through it all, sound asleep on a cushion. They finally woke him and said to him ‘Teacher, does it not matter to you that we are going to drown. He awoke and rebuked the wind and said to the sea: ‘Quiet! Be still!’”

Again, the minister looked at those in the funeral home, “It may appear that God isn’t doing anything. Fear might replace faith, however, Jesus hears our cries and responds.”

The minister then returned to reading from the bible, “The wind fell off and everything grew calm. Then he said to them, ‘Why are you so terrified? Why are you so lacking in faith?’”

Again, the minister stopped reading and spoke directly, “Yes, friends, sudden storms allow us to turn to Jesus, and such storms will not last forever. God will assist.”

Reading again from the Bible, the minister said, “A great awe overcame them at this. They kept saying to one another, ‘Who can this be that the wind and the sea obey him?’”

The minister closed with, “The disciples were overwhelmed by what they had heard and seen. They now had a reverential fear of Jesus, and thus, my friends when sudden bad things happen, we need to remember that God is in control. With this thought and prayer, let us take Oscar to his place of rest.”

With that, everyone in the funeral home stood as the pallbearers lifted the casket and took it outside to the waiting hearse. During this time, Parker again was aware that the stranger in a dark blue suit who kept nervously touching his mustache was also keeping a close watch of all the people in attendance but with a particular attention on Edward, who in turn kept his gaze on the casket as it was moved from the center of the funeral parlor to the waiting outside hearse.

Once outside, cars slowly pulled in behind the hearse as the funeral line for the drive to Woodlawn Cemetery started to form. Parker walked around the sidewalks watching everything while being aware of mustache who hailed a cab, which then drove off in a different direction. Mustache wasn’t going to the cemetery, and Parker wondered why he was at the funeral. Perhaps he knew Oscar from the past, but it seemed that he was there to observe the funeral and note the various people in attendance. Parker then started to speculate about Mustache’s purpose, but he quickly stopped himself knowing that speculation without facts was not helpful and many times led to incorrect conclusions. Besides, Parker could console himself for the moment with the sermon he had just heard, which had ended with the words that God is in control.

(11) The Murray Family Interviews

At the Shakespeare police station, Parker sat with two Chicago police officers, one a man and the other a woman, in a darkened side room that had a large mirror allowing them to view the bright interview room next door. In that room sat Detective Sergeant Michael Boyle, Detective Brendan, and a female police stenographer. John Murray was ushered in and sat opposite Boyle. Behind Boyle on the wall was a mirror. John Murray could see himself in the mirror and the back of Boyle's head; however, this was a one-way mirror and on the other side, hidden to John Murray sat Parker and the two police officers. Boyle was using the Shakespeare office because of the one-way mirror. His Damen Avenue headquarters did not have such a mirror.

The interview went quickly. John said he and Ruthy bought the house in the early 1950's and rented out the upstairs flat where Oscar was murdered. Their tenants before Oscar were a young couple who suddenly and unexpectedly came into money by winning a lottery, allowing them to buy a house in a western suburb of Chicago. At the same time, Oscar was looking for an apartment, heard about the upcoming vacancy, and just like that the Murray's had a new tenant. All this happened quickly and the upstairs was never vacant because a day after the couple moved out, Oscar moved in. Before all of this happened, Edward, the son of John's older brother, had been given a key to the two-family house and started visiting them on weekends. Once inside the house there were stairs that went up to Oscar's apartment, but Edward used the small spare bedroom in John and Ruthy's apartment when he came into the city to party on weekends. Edward had his own apartment in Lemont, a southwest suburb of Chicago, where he worked at the Argonne National Laboratory. John was not clear about what Edward did at Argonne except that Edward had his M.S. in physics and worked on communication devices. John also said everything went smoothly for the year that Oscar was a tenant and then came the shock of his murder.

After John's interview, it was Ruthy's turn, and she answered all the questions exactly the way John had answered them. When asked about Edward using her spare bedroom on weekends, she said the young man was a delight and added a spark to the household on those weekends when he was around, which was frequently but not every weekend. She added that Edward spent his weekend evenings at O'Rourke's, a tavern on North Avenue, that attracted a number of Chicago and even Hollywood celebrities along with well-educated but somewhat unconventional individuals.

Finally, it was Edward's turn to be interviewed. Edward said he met Oscar several weeks after Oscar had moved into the apartment. Their contact was limited, usually a hello greeting or some trivial comment about the weather. Edward claimed that he and Oscar never had a conversation of any substance. Moreover, Edward said he had never been in Oscar's apartment, did not know what Oscar did for a living, and never told Oscar that he worked at Argonne. With respect to his job, Edward refused to talk about it, claiming he could not do so because some of his work was classified. Edward said he didn't have a girlfriend. He kept in touch with his university classmates both males and females and developed intellectual friendships with a number of folks who gathered on Friday and Saturday nights at O'Rourke's tavern on North Avenue, which was about a mile north of downtown Chicago.

After the three Murray's had left the police station, Michael and Parker talked about the case. It appeared strange to Parker that Oscar, living upstairs, was a complete stranger to the Murray's. The apartment suddenly became available because the original renting couple won a lottery giving them the down payment they needed on a house they wanted. Then Oscar suddenly appears and immediately moves into the newly available apartment. He lives there quietly and then is murdered by having his throat cut.

"All of that combined together is unusual," said Parker.

Michael agreed and said initially he didn't know what to make of it but now the case had changed even more because of a new development. Michael then told his son-in-law that Frank Jenkins, who headed the Central Intelligence Agency in Miami, was visiting the Damen Avenue police station tomorrow to talk to them about Oscar because Oscar was an employee of the CIA, which was "almost certainly the reason for his murder" and that Frank Jenkins wanted Parker to be at the meeting since he was aware that Parker helped his father-in-law on various cases. With that, Parker realized that his early involvement in Oscar's murder meant he was now involved in a national security murder because obscure Oscar was really a "CIA spy" that had been assassinated. Moreover, what Parker had just called unusual perhaps had an explanation. That is, Parker recognized that the lucky couple who won money that enabled them to move perhaps were *picked* to win so that they would move and then Oscar could move into that apartment and better watch that neighborhood and perhaps the Murray's nephew, Edward.

Moreover, as both the Sergeant and Parker knew, the CIA was sometimes involved with unusual or weird things that weren't completely understood. Parker's sudden unexplained insights, which were essentially correct, was something that Parker didn't understand. Apparently, the CIA was already aware that Parker had such insights and that these insights helped the police solve cases.

"I gather you haven't had one of your "flashes" or "insights" when it comes to Oscar's murder?" asked the father-in-law.

"No, nothing yet. As you're aware, they just suddenly happen, and I'm aware of something that has occurred or is occurring, but it's never 100% clear, sometimes far from it, but usually I'm able to piece things together that I wouldn't have been able to do without the benefit of the insight or flash that somehow does illuminate reality."

"Yea, well it seems that the CIA is aware of this phenomenon which helps you to solve cases and has asked that you attend tomorrow's session."

"I wouldn't miss it," replied Parker. "Given the CIA involvement, this case has just become a touch out of the ordinary and may continue to have unconventional ties."

(12) The CIA Gets Involved

The next afternoon Parker and Detective Brendan joined Sergeant Boyle at the Area 6 Homicide Unit on Damen Avenue. For privacy, the Sergeant booked the small conference room on the first floor for the meeting rather than using his desk, which was out in the open on the third floor. The three men were there early and sat in the room waiting for Frank Jenkins.

"Do we know anything about Frank Jenkins other than he runs the Miami CIA office and had Oscar here in Chicago on his payroll?" asked Parker.

"Frank's title is Special Agent, Central Intelligence Agency, and yes, he's in charge of their Miami office. The CIA is a civilian intelligence service tasked with advancing national security through collecting and analyzing intelligence from around the world," replied the Sergeant reading from his file, "and they're involved in conducting covert operations. Apparently, Oscar was on their payroll and passed information to them."

"I have Oscar's black book here," said Parker. "You gave the Special Agent's name as Frank Jenkins, and that probably explains the FJ who sent Oscar monthly payments of $2,500, or $30,000 a year, according to the black book."

"Not a bad salary in 1972 for a man who spent most of his time giving odds on sporting events," remarked the Sergeant with Detective Brendan vigorously nodding his head in agreement. Thirty grand a year was triple to what a Chicago police office earned!

At exactly 1 pm, Frank Jenkins, six feet tall with a well-defined ruddy face and very blue eyes, arrived. He opened his briefcase, removed three folders, and after introductions handed each participant a folder. "Gentlemen, thank you, for having this meeting. Oscar Busby worked for our Agency. He had contact with individuals who might be spying on the United States and passing secrets to foreign powers. We believe Oscar recently identified a person who he thought was a Soviet spy and was about to give us that person's name and the specifics of a crime. That's the likely reason for his murder. We believe the suspect discovered Oscar's undercover work and had him murdered. Now each folder that I just handed out contains the same information, thus each of you has identical information for your research. Within each folder there on nine packets, one for each individual that's a current suspect in spying for the Soviet Union: five of the packets are for men who frequent Chicago race tracks, another packet is for a very active chess player who also plays in Europe, and the remaining three packets are skilled men who work in different professions including the nephew of Oscar's landlord who is employed at Argonne National Laboratory along with two lawyers who work for different international firms recruiting new employees."

At this point, Jenkins turned toward the Sergeant. "I hope, Sergeant Boyle, that your Homicide Unit investigating the murder of Oscar Busby will focus on this information and see if you discover anything. Remember each of these men are only suspects of being spies and for passing information to the Soviets. Even if some of them are spies, it doesn't mean that one of them killed Oscar. However, their spying could be the reason for Oscar's death since he was about to name a spy. Finally, if there is anything you can add to the file, even if it seems minor, please include it. Also, if anything seems to be incorrect, please mention it. I would appreciate a telephone call at least once a week to update me, even if there's no progress. Please take a few minutes to look at the information on each of the men who are suspected of spying for a foreign power."

Parker looked at each of the packets and recognized only two names: Barry Snyder, the chess player from Gompers Park, who was one of the leaders of the Gompers Park Chess Club, and Edward Murray, John Murray's nephew, who had a key to the house where Oscar was murdered.

Parker opened Edward's packet first. It showed that his profession was a Staff Scientist at Argonne National Laboratory. This packet contained several photographs of Edward surrounded by a large computer and technical laboratory equipment. It indicated that he was developing 'an electronic translator of cetacean sounds'. Parker knew cetaceans were sea dwelling mammals but wondered what the device was. It appeared that the device was an attempt to understand the squeals of dolphins. Apparently, most of Edward's work on this project was classified, and it had been leaked, making Edward a suspect.

The Barry Snyder packet showed him to be an insurance executive wearing a suit and tie and seated at a desk and then photographs of him playing chess in various European cities and then photographs of him next to various European men, none of whom Parker recognized as being famous. It was unclear if these men were insurance executives or chess players but looking at the photos, it was likely that everyone in the photos played chess and those wearing ties were the insurance executives in their work clothes. In any case, Barry had too many chess friends who were connected to the KGB, which was also known as the Committee for State Security. This Committee was responsible for the removal of Alexander Dubcek and the Prague Spring in 1968 Czechoslovakia. Four years later, the removal of Dubcek and crushing the Prague Spring was still a rallying cry against the Soviets and their KGB or Komitet Gosudarstvennoy Bezopssnosti throughout most of Europe.

Sergeant Boyle looked at the list of names and said, "I recognize some of these names. We already have files on the five men who follow horse racing. Do you want copies of these files?"

"Yes," said Jenkins, "and the person who handles all such material at our Miami Office is Miss Aurelia Qundo. Hearing the name, Parker was surprised. He knew the name Aurelia Qundo from four years ago when she was visiting Chicago during the 1968 Democratic Party Convention with a group of students. That's such a rare name; it has to be her thought Parker. He recalled he was impressed with Aurelia's intelligence as he helped her while she calmly prevented her students from protesting in Grant Park the night when the downtown area erupted into riots. Unknown to Parker was that Aurelia back then worked at a sea mammal research lab while finishing her Ph.D., and she had just delivered a lecture on cetaceans to these summer students.

"Here's a photo of Aurelia Qundo," continued Jenkins and with that, he produced a colored photo of Aurelia – a beautiful woman in her twenties with long golden hair and brown eyes. Parker looked at the photo and confirmed it was the Aurelia he knew from 1968, four years ago. Her hair was shorter in the photo, but the face and hair color were unmistakable.

"You know what I look like so I'm not giving you a photo of me," continued a smiling Jenkins, "However, and this is important, should I or Aurelia ever call you on the telephone or write to you we will start the conversation by using the words 'small apple'. If you don't hear or see those words up front, it's not us. Also, you should use the code 'small apple' when you write to us or call either of us on the telephone so that we know it's really you. This may seem childish, but we've found a simple code like this an effective tool."

The Sergeant, Detective Brendan, and Parker all nodded to Special Agent Jenkins that they understood him. "Do you have any questions for me?" asked Jenkins.

"Yes," said Sergeant Boyle, "I don't see Susan Danford's name on your list, yet Oscar was dating her several weeks earlier this year, and they split up according to her after a trip to Florida because he wouldn't marry her. She's on my list because her fresh fingerprints were found in Oscar's apartment, and she lied to me saying that she hadn't been in his place since April."

"The Agency learned about Miss Danford from Oscar last January. We checked her out back then and found nothing of concern. I wasn't aware that they had separated. We'll investigate this development and let you know if we discover anything. Thank you, for this information."

The Sergeant, after looking at Detective Brendan, indicated that he didn't have anything more to say. Thus, Parker holding the black book in his hand said, "Oscar took bets from anyone who wanted to place one and wrote everything in a black book. We don't have the black book he was using the night he was murdered, but this black book is the prior one. When you look at it, you'll observe that no full names are used – usually it's the first name initial and a last name initial; however, Oscar's book lists everyone who did business with him from October of last year through mid-April this year. For example, Oscar received $2,500 monthly, a tidy sum, from FJ. It's possible that the murderer's initials are also here. Do you want the book?"

Frank Jenkins, without acknowledging or denying that he was the FJ listed, took the book and began looking through it. "This is very detailed – certainly don't throw it out. If you have a clerk here at Area 6 Homicide, perhaps the clerk could take the nine names on my list and record the number of times their initials appear in this book. If you don't have a clerk to handle this kind of detailed work, then I don't know if it's worth hiring someone to do this work or not. Clearly, if the killer never made bets, his initials are not going to be in the book. I'd say that you should investigate my nine names first as I indicated and see if something develops, but don't throw this book away. If we're able to close in on one of the men listed in your packets, then checking if he placed bets with Oscar would be worth the effort." With that, Jenkins returned the book to Parker and looked at the other two detectives. They didn't have anything further to say, and Parker decided not to say anything about meeting Aurelia Qundo four years ago, and thus, everyone shook hands and the meeting was over.

As Jenkins was leaving the room, he motioned to Parker and handed him a card, "Mr. Spooner, we have heard that you are a person that sometimes experiences insights into future events that are useful in your detective investigations. Our agency is using some new technology to scan a person's body and brain to see if we can detect any special signal coming from the brain of that person. If you're willing to participate in such studies, please call Miss Aurelia Qundo at the number on this second card. It's a different phone number than the other phone number you have for her. This is a separate study we've started, and she'll provide you with all the information." With that Jenkins again shook Parker's hand and quickly bounded out of the police station.

Parker stood there, looking at the card. He thought about calling Aurelia in the future, remembering her from the past, and having just heard her name in the present. This triple injunction of Aurelia's name from the past, present, and future resonated with him, and suddenly a new *insight* flashed in Parker's mind. Parker now knew and was thinking, "*Aurelia Qundo and I will be involved in solving Oscar's murder and the revelation of a secret.*"

With this insight, Parker had to sit down. As far as subjecting himself to tests that would scan his body and brain in an attempt to determine the nature of these insights, Parker decided that he wouldn't do it. His insights were rare and passed quickly. In order to be detected, Parker would have to be connected to the measuring equipment continuously for various periods of time, which was not possible, and it wasn't even known if such insights could be detected by the particular equipment employed for that task.

Parker's mind then thought about Frank Jenkins and the non-military civilian structured CIA. He wondered if Jenkins accomplished all of what he had intended to accomplish by his visit to the Damen Avenue police station. Parker wouldn't have been surprised that Special Agent Jenkins had scheduled other meetings in Chicago, and that his upcoming flight was the last one out of O'Hare for that day, and it was a private jet to Langley, Virginia.

Frank's next meeting was with two officials from the Argonne National Laboratory, and it took place at The Berghoff, a legendary German restaurant in the Loop. It was midafternoon and the place wasn't crowded. The three men took a table at the rear of the restaurant and ordered ice teas. One of the Argonne men sported a beard, while the other wore glasses.

After verifying Frank's identity, Beard said, "Edward Murray worked on a classified project which developed a way of possibly communicating with highly developed sea mammals such as dolphins. A portion of that project was leaked and wound up in the hands of the Soviet Union. We don't know for certain, but some evidence indicates that Edward was responsible, either intentionally or inadvertently for the leak. He's no longer working on anything that's classified. We understood that the CIA was involved in his case, and we've been waiting for an update on his involvement, if any, in the leak."

Glasses quickly added, "The murder of Oscar Busby in the house where Edward lives when he goes to Chicago on weekends is obviously of concern to us. Is there anything you can tell us about that household or Edward?"

"John and Ruthy Murray are homeowners who rent out their upstairs apartment," replied Frank Jenkins. "They are not a threat to the United States. Their nephew, Edward Murray, *may have passed* Argonne information to the Soviets. We are *not* certain about that. The Agency was able to insert Oscar into the Murray household's apartment to watch Edward and other events on the north side of Chicago. Oscar had found nothing amiss with Edward, who may be laying low; however, Oscar was onto someone else and was getting close to finding evidence and naming that individual as a Soviet spy. We believe that's why he was murdered."

"Thus, Edward most likely had nothing to do with Oscar's murder, but you're uncertain if he leaked our information or not?" asked Beard.

"That's correct," replied Frank.

"With respect to Edward then, what would you recommend that we do with him?" asked Glasses.

"Do nothing, right now. Oscar's murder investigation has just started. Edward should continue at his current job but watch him. If he does something wrong or if he did something wrong in the past that you're able to document, then act. In the same way, if the CIA comes across some wrongdoing that impacts Argonne, then we will immediately provide you with the facts. If you find that Edward's guilty of anything internally, I know you will act according to your procedures, and if that happens, then you should inform the CIA as to what you discovered about Edward." With that said, Frank Jenkins finished his iced tea, excused himself, and quickly went off to his next meeting.

Frank's third meeting was at a CIA safe house on Chicago's lakefront. He had ordered Bob Hanson to move there after Oscar's murder. Frank wasn't about to lose a second agent to an unknown killer, saying "We're sending you to Reykjavik, Iceland for the upcoming world chess championship between Bobby Fischer and Boris Spassky. The cover story is that you recently came into money through the death of a distant relative. We'll help you to simultaneously send this news to all your friends and relatives just as your plane to Reykjavik is about to leave, which I expect to be in three days. This message will stop people from looking for you and wondering what happened to you. You'll stay in Reykjavik for the duration of the match, which should be at least through August. We'll keep you posted if we apprehend the killer earlier. Is there anyone that you have to see before you leave?"

Bob was used to Frank's rapid-fire delivery and thought something like this was going to happen when he was told to go hide at the safe house the morning after Oscar's murder was known. "I would like to see Susan Danford," was Bob's request.

Frank frowned, "I don't think that can happen. Susan's role, if any, in Oscar's murder hasn't been established. There's even likelihood that she was in Oscar's apartment the night of the murder. Why do you want to see her?"

"I like her, Frank. I believe she was crushed when she found out about Oscar's death. I don't think she knew he was working as a CIA agent, but apparently, she saw enough on her Florida trip with Oscar to realize that she couldn't have a normal life with him, and thus she stopped seeing him."

"It's very likely that Oscar's April trip to Miami tipped others off as to his role in the Agency. At one point he had a scheduled meeting with Miss Qundo. We arranged that meeting before he left, and there never was any other contact between us and Oscar while he was in Florida. However, if someone was watching him in Florida, then our meeting with Oscar probably led them to us, the CIA. In brief, we sadly think his trip with Susan last April to Miami may have led to his murder," said Frank. "In any case, your request to see Susan is denied."

"Okay, then I can't and won't see her. She'll just be one of the many chess players to receive a message of my good fortune at inheriting money and going off to enjoy the world chess championship match." Bob was both sad and somewhat angry with Frank's decision.

"Yes," replied Frank quickly catching Bob's mood, "however, since you asked to see her, we'll add, 'I'll see you as soon as I return' to Susan's message. That will definitely show Susan that you're thinking about her." Bob smiled. This was classic Frank Jenkins. He was accommodating Bob's request somewhat, and although Frank didn't say it directly, Bob knew that Jenkins hadn't completely ruled out the possibility that Susan Danford was the person who cut Oscar's throat and that was the reason he denied Bob's request.

Finally, Frank had one more thing to discuss with Bob and that was Barry Snyder. "What's the latest on Barry and his relationship with Lieutenant Gary Cambe?" he asked.

"I've nothing different to say except to confirm what I've already reported. Their wives are sisters, and the families see each other because of that connection. Additionally, the two men, Barry Snyder and Lieutenant Gary Cambe, sometimes play golf together. They talk as they ride around in their golf cart, and you can see that there's an exchange of papers. We would have to have a listening device implanted into their golf cart to hear if it's classified information that's going back and forth or just talking about their golf routine. Almost always after they play golf, Barry goes to Europe for a chess tournament where he talks to Russian players. This could be a possible conduit of secrets going back and forth between the Soviets and the United States."

"Is there any indication that Oscar discovered something important regarding this potential spying and was about to reveal it?'

“If that’s the case, Oscar didn’t say anything to me,” said Bob sadly, thinking of Oscar’s death.

“What about Pavel Kotov?” asked Frank. “He’s related to the two sisters.”

“They’re first cousins – the women had the Kotov last name before their marriages, but the ladies or their husbands don’t appear to be close to Pavel in any way. Pavel’s single and apparently merely just another male chess player at Gompers Park. In brief, the fact that Barry Snyder’s wife and Pavel are first cousins doesn’t seem to be a dynamic in any potential spying on Pavel’s part.”

“Thank you for clarifying the situation, Bob. Once you get settled in at Reykjavik, write a brief report for CIA files on these relationships. Enjoy the world champion chess match” and with that Frank shook Bob Hansen’s hand as he raced to the airport.

(13) Lt. Cambe's Complaint

Lieutenant Gary Cambe was annoyed by Frank Jenkins and the CIA and complained to everyone in the chain of command at the Chicago Police Department. He was annoyed that he knew nothing of the CIA's direct visit to the Homicide Unit of Area 6 regarding the murder of Oscar Busby. It was true that Oscar's murder did fall under the jurisdiction of that Homicide Unit, but the Lieutenant argued that the CIA should have started the investigation at a higher level given the potential adverse national implications for Chicago that a CIA employee had been murdered in the city. The Lieutenant only learned of the crime when Sergeant Boyle sent the information that his unit was now investigating nine individuals as potential spies of a foreign adversary. Lieutenant Cambe immediately told Sergeant Boyle that any information gathered by Area 6 Homicide on these potential spies had to be sent to him before acting on any response.

Lieutenant Cambe's complaint made its way up to the Superintendent of Police, who told him they had periodic meetings with the Central Intelligence Agency in Langley, Virginia, and this topic would be discussed at their next meeting. Cambe rolled his eyes – the CIA would hear about it, but Cambe knew nothing was going to happen to Jenkins and the way he operated.

The investigation of the nine men as potential spies that Jenkins had identified amused Cambe. First, there were five race track gamblers that had been known to Chicago police for some time. They dealt with all types of people but not surprisingly they were all folks that gambled. They frequented Las Vegas and Atlantic City. The chances of any of them being a serious spy for some foreign power were

slim. Then there were two lawyers from two separate international law firms.
They didn't know each other but both of them seemed to recruit younger people who had just graduated from top law schools. These recruiters were always at functions and parties looking for talent.

Undoubtedly, each of these recruiters at some time crossed the path of a person who might be some sort of security risk to the United States, and thus the names of such recruiters may have worked their way onto Jenkins's list.

Next there was Edward Murray, a young man with University of Chicago degrees working at Argonne National Laboratory in Lemont Illinois. He had a high level of clearance but one of the projects that he was responsible for was leaked to the Soviet Union. Edward might have taken money or something of value for that information.

Lieutenant Cambe was shaking his head and laughing at this list. The Lieutenant felt that legitimate spies had nothing to worry about if this was the best the CIA could do in identifying them. However, he stopped laughing when he came to the last name on the list. It was Barry Snyder, a middle-aged, top notch chess player, and insurance executive, who spoke Russian and played in European Chess Tournaments. Barry knew many Russians and may have intentionally or inadvertently passed some sensitive information on one of his trips. This too on the surface could have been laughable. Barry Snyder spoke Russian and played chess so of course he knew Russian chess players!

However, not contained in this report was the fact that Barry Snyder and Lieutenant Gary Cambe were connected because *their wives were sisters*. Vera Kotov married Gary

Cambe right out of high school and soon thereafter Vernonica Kotov and Barry Snyder married. Barry and the Lieutenant were brothers-in-law and as such occasionally played a round of golf besides sharing holidays together. This CIA report didn't say anything about this relationship, but any future investigation would quickly reveal it, and this – the fact that his brother-in-law, Barry Snyder, was on the CIA watch list - bothered the Lieutenant.

At this moment, the Lieutenant was told that Miss Marsha Dempsey had arrived for the interview that he requested. The Lieutenant placed the CIA report into his desk as Marsha entered his office. She wore a very short skirt and a low-cut blouse. The Lieutenant was not that surprised by her streetwalker appearance but by the way she spoke, which indicated a surprising intelligence. His mind became excited at her presence as a smart young good-looking woman.

"I imagine you wish to talk about one of my friends, Michael Klossmeier," said Marsha taking a seat in front of the Lieutenant's desk.

"Yes, I'm interested in him and hope, Miss Demsey, that you're able to provide some information about him." There was no doubt that the Lieutenant was also interested in Marsha as he continued to stare at her. Marsha felt that he had begun the process of mentally undressing her.

"Michael is a friend of mine, and I'm not a person that talks about friends to strangers," replied Marsha looking away from the Lieutenant's gaze.

"I'm a police Lieutenant and looking for information. I'm not a stranger. Michael seems to have come into some money recently. Have you noticed his new money?" She's also a feisty woman given her response thought the Lieutenant becoming more excited at her presence.

“Michael has recently moved to Madison Wisconsin. I think he intends to buy a house,” replied Marsha ignoring his question about money. She didn’t like this man and felt uncomfortable as he stared at her. Her mother had cautioned her about dressing inappropriately because many men were looking for an easy woman, but Marsha had not been paying attention to her mother.

The Lieutenant sat back in his chair. “Will you be joining him up there if that happens, and he does buy a house?” Cambe was now smiling at that thought.

“I don’t know. I don’t know anything about his plans except he seems anxious to put his past behind him and start over.” Marsha’s eyes moved around the room to avoid Lieutenant Cambe’s annoying gaze.

“You’re aware that Klossmeier was in prison for the stabbing he committed when he was only 18 years old? Cambe wondered if Marsha realized that Mic had displayed aggression in the past.

“Yes, I know that, but that’s Michael’s past. As I said before, he’s starting over.” Marsha was now firmly looking at Cambe.

“And you’re there to help him?”

“Perhaps, if I’m able. I certainly don’t want him to get into any more trouble. Are we done here?” Marsha asked, continuing now to look directly at the Lieutenant in an unfriendly way.

"One more question, Miss Dempsey, do you know the source of Michael's money?"

"What do you mean, the source of his money? I thought his family always had it."

"Well, yes, of course, Miss Dempsey, that makes sense," replied the Lieutenant. "It's fortunate to have a boyfriend who isn't poor, and I wish you the best." He smiled as he walked Marsha to the door, putting his hand on her shoulder. Marsha walked faster and was out the door quickly, forcing his hand to fall to his side. She was happy to be free of this man and quickly walked away, not looking back.

The Lieutenant thought it was interesting that Mic was settling down and had now found himself a woman who believed that Mic always had money. Mic was a lucky man to have attracted a hot woman like Marsha, but she was way too smart and feisty for him. The attraction would never last between them thought Cambe, and Marsha would be looking for a better man soon. The Lieutenant decided he would carefully watch what developed for Mic in Madison, Wisconsin.

Marsha, meanwhile, was thinking about what her mother, Delia, had warned her about which was the inappropriate way Marsha dressed. By revealing too much, Marsha would be sending the wrong message to men who only had sex on their mind. Marsha scoffed at this and said she could handle any situation. However, when older men in authority like the police Lieutenant started eyeing Marsha, she became upset and annoyed. Perhaps her mother had made a valid point, and Marsha would have to change how she dressed in order to avoid being annoyed by men who were not worthy of her time.

(14) Susan Danford's Decision

After Oscar's funeral, Susan Danford was in a state of panic. Sergeant Boyle wanted her to return to the police station to answer further questions. She knew it had to be that her fingerprints were found in Oscar's apartment. She never should have agreed to having her fingerprints taken because *she was in Oscar's apartment the night he was murdered.* Oscar had telephoned her and begged her to come to the apartment that night. She agreed and once there, he apologized for taking her to Florida last April. He couldn't discuss his work, but it was dangerous and he had inadvertently and inappropriately involved her. He said he was sorry and gave Susan a pair of earrings. Susan was surprised and quickly accepted both the apology and the gift. Oscar then gave Susan his current black book. He said this book was slightly different from prior ones because it had additional information. If something happened to him, he asked Susan to give the book to Bob Hanson. Above all, it was important that the black book did not fall into the hands of the police because some of the police were corrupt and could not be trusted. Susan didn't fully understand, but she agreed to take the black book and give it to Bob Hanson, not the police, should something happen to Oscar.

She left Oscar's apartment Thursday night confused and frightened. The next morning her worst fear was realized when she learned of Oscar's murder. She looked at the pages in the black book, and its contents appeared similar to the prior book that she had seen Oscar use before. Only the back cover was different. There, the word ANAGRAM, all in capitals, was printed. She knew what an anagram was but couldn't relate the word to anything she was seeing, and she didn't see anything else in the black book except the usual bets that Oscar recorded along with payouts made and money collected.

When the police interviewed her on Saturday afternoon after the murder, she didn't mention the meeting with Oscar and having his black book because Oscar had been quite adamant that the book should not be given to the corrupt police. She expected to give the black book to Bob Hanson as instructed by Oscar, but Bob wasn't at Oscar's wake or funeral. Bob was missing, and the police were looking for him. Susan didn't know what to do. She waited, thinking Bob would contact her but then she along with many chess players received a note saying Bob had inherited money and was off to Reykjavik for the Fischer-Spassky world chess championship.

She didn't believe Bob had inherited money. As Susan rethought Oscar's last meeting with her immediately before his murder and then their Florida breakup in April, she remembered both Boris with his Russian accent and the beautiful woman in her white Mercides. She now realized that Oscar was likely dealing with international crimes and possibly spies. With these thoughts, Susan became frightened. She recognized that she might be in danger and had to get rid of the black book! Susan promised Oscar that she wouldn't give it to the *corrupt* police, but Parker Spooner was present at her Saturday afternoon police interview, and he wasn't police. Additionally, Parker knew Bob and the other chess players at Gompers Park. Thus, in an instant, Susan decided to mail the black book to Parker with a note, 'Oscar said <u>not</u> to give this book to the corrupt police.' Susan did not sign the note and mailed the black book to Parker without a return address. She then packed a suitcase and left Chicago on a bus for a trip to Miami. She kept thinking about the beautiful woman in the white convertible with the golden hair and the man 'Boris Volkov' who had occupied Oscar's time in Miami. They had ruined her relationship with Oscar and probably were involved in his murder. She would have to be careful, but Susan was determined to locate and gather information about them.

(15) Grace Graduates

Father Joseph spoke at Grace's graduation at an all-girls high school on Chicago's south side. Grace quickly wrote down the priest's opening which she found inspirational knowing that she would soon forget it if she didn't record it immediately. The priest said according to Grace's shorthand, "High School graduation is a watershed moment for many young ladies. Some are now engaged to be married. Some will be off to college. Some will join the country's work force, while two are joining convents that help the poor. Regardless of where you go, your four years at Sacred Heart will remain a solid foundation for further growth and hope for the Church and the future of humanity. What you do in the future, how you conduct yourself from now on is important not only to you and those who you love and their love for you but for the good of the Body of Christ and eventually for *everyone* who struggles to live a good and holy life." Grace was uplifted by these words because this was an example of what her father, Parker Spooner, called 'the coherence of Catholicism.'

After the graduation ceremony, the Parker Spooner family had a photograph taken: the mother, Rosemary; older brother, John; younger brother Peter; younger sister, Anna; along with Parker, the father, who stood next to daughter Grace for her high school graduation family picture. The family then went to one of Grace's favorite restaurants, for a graduation dinner. They were joined by Grandpa and Grandma Boyle and Parker's mother, Nana, who baby sat the grandkids many times. Parker's father had died many years ago, but the family remembered him on these special occasions and always in their prayers.

During the dinner, Parker announced a family vacation to Florida to visit Disney World. In October 1971, Walt

Disney World opened its Magic Kingdom near Orlando, Florida, and Rosemary and Parker decided take their four children there to celebrate not only Grace's high school graduation but also John's high school graduation, which had happened a year before the new theme park opened. Parker's plan was to drive from Chicago to Orlando in their station wagon, which easily held the six of them and had a luggage facility on the car's roof. The driving distance from Chicago to Orlando was over 1,100 miles and would require a one night stay in a motel both going and returning, which should be easy to do with both Parker and Rosemary sharing the driving and having both John and Grace with their driver's licenses for backup.

"I'm going to buy new shorts and tops with my graduation money," said Grace excitedly. "What about you John?"

"I need a new pair of tennis shoes and have the money. Let me know when you want to go shopping."

"When do you see us leaving for Orlando, Dad?" asked Grace.

"Your mother and I were thinking about early Saturday, July 8, arriving late Sunday at Disney World. I think we can get close to the northern part of Georgia the first day of driving and make mass Sunday morning somewhere in Atlanta and then arrive Sunday night at the Magic Kingdom. I plan to make the reservations at the Kingdom tomorrow."

"That's great, Dad. We can make that drive easily because I'm comfortable with driving, if needed," said John.

"Wow! This is fantastic, Mom and Dad! I'll be the first kid in my class to see Disney World," said an excited Peter, looking up from his chess board.

"Will Mickey and Minny be there?" asked Anna, "I see them on TV in California, but will they be in Florida?"

"Yes, sweetheart, all the Disney characters will be in Florida," said the mother.

"What about poor Bambi?" said Anna. She was very upset by the movie where Bambi's mother had been shot.

"Bambi is grown up now and doing fine, Anna, do not worry. You'll see him," said Rosemary, glancing at Parker. Parker had told his wife that the late Walt Disney had done wonders with his creations but the negative impact on young children of Bambi's mother being killed by hunters was one of the few criticisms of his work. Parker also wondered how families in the future would handle the upcoming technology revolutions that were certain to bring the ugly side of life to young minds. Rosemary was a touch more optimistic, at least long term. She told Parker that women would continue to bite into bad apples but as evil effects spread and became manifest more women would recognize their importance in human life and work to stop harmful effects.

Later that night, after the grandparents had gone home and as the Spooners were about to retire, Grace, seeing that their bedroom light was still on, knocked on her parents' door, "Mother and Father," she said.

"Come in, Grace," said Rosemary.

Grace walked into their bedroom, "Mother and Father, I want to thank you for my wonderful birthday. I'm so happy to have made it through high school and for all the time and love you have shown me. I'm one of the luckiest kids to have you as my parents," and with that she kissed her mother and then her father before running out of the room and closing the door.

"You did a good job raising her, Rosemary."

"You helped, Parker. You were home every night, and the kids saw you. In spite of your actuarial consulting work and being a private detective on the side, you were here to help me raise our children. I don't think Grace would have come in here tonight if you hadn't been by my side every day of every year of her life."

Parker nodded his agreement, "I sense the same is true with John. He may not be that expressive, but if you read the birthday cards he has given us, it's the same message."

"Yes, you're correct. Both of our teenagers now recognize us as good parents. We're blessed."

The parents embraced, turned off the light, and holding hands went into their marriage bed.

(16) The Brookfield Zoo

Rosemary had her monthly luncheon with her lady friends; John was taking his finals at the University of Chicago; and all the other kids, Grace, Peter, and Anna, were finished with school allowing Parker to take them on a weekday visit to the Brookfield Zoo. They paid for a tour of the dolphin aquariums, and a young woman, Kaitleen, was their guide. She invited people to ask questions as they moved around the extensive facilities. Their first stop was a giant aquarium that was two stories tall, and several bottle-neck dolphins came down to the ground level allowing the crowd of people to view them.

"Dolphins belong to a group called Cetaceans, which is entirely an aquatic group of mammals including whales and porpoises," said Kaitleen. "Cetaceans breathe air, give birth to live young, produce milk, and have hair—all features of mammals. Because of their body form, however, cetaceans were commonly grouped with fish. This is unfortunate because some species of dolphins have impressive cognitive abilities and are capable of understanding complex concepts. They learn to understand human commands and respond to them. They mimic human speech, have a high level of language comprehension, a strong sense of spatial awareness, and can navigate through complex environments."

Parker raised his hand and asked, "Do you think they are self-aware?"

"Yes, our research indicates they have a high level of self-awareness. They certainly are capable of recognizing themselves in mirrors, which is a trait that is only found in a few other species, including great apes, elephants, and of course, humans," answered Kaitleen, who placed her hand on the enormous sized tank. Two dolphins immediately moved up to the glass to acknowledge her gesture.

"They recognize me," explained Kaitleen. "Dolphins are highly social animals, and they have been observed displaying a range of emotions. They're capable of forming strong bonds with other dolphins and as you just saw with these two dolphins, they know me as a human."

"Have you in some way bonded with them?" asked Parker.

"Not with most of them in this tank but with these two, yes. I believe if I fell into their tank and needed help, I would have it from them. I've also seen other dolphins display empathy and help an injured dolphin. I also know that all these mammals display that they are not only alive, but they're aware of their environment and have emotions. Moreover, they exhibit self-controlled behavior, seem to have personalities, and treat other dolphins appropriately, perhaps ethically. When it comes to what defines a person, dolphins definitely have it," said Kaitleen with conviction.

Another man who had been shaking his head sideways raised his hand and asked, "So you're saying they're intelligent, yet they haven't any technology."

"Well, people think of intelligence as the harnessing of technology, and the ability to think abstractly as achieving growth and progress. These thoughts have made it easy for humans to reject the concept of intelligence in other species. But what if a species didn't need human technology to thrive; rather, what if that "technology" was already latent or built within that species?" stated Kaitleen raising this possibility.

The man continued to look skeptical, so Kaitleen smiled and continued, "If we examine the brains of one of the smartest groups of animals, the cetaceans are right there. The quality of their brain tissue is somewhat different from humans, and that makes it challenging to quantify. However, certain species of dolphins host sonar-like devices and are able to use sonar to actually see the internal workings of other animals similar to ultrasound used in human medicine. Studies have shown they use this ability to read emotions and states of health."

"It sounds like you rank them quite high in rating species by intelligence, which usually has apes ranking behind humans," said Parker.

"Both humans and apes are land based. In the oceans, you have whales, octopuses, and seals along with dolphins. It's difficult to evaluate intelligence because of the different environments of land and sea, but I think dolphins are at the top behind humans because they have remarkable communication abilities, most of which aren't understood by us. Remember they live in the ocean and it's dark down there. We need lights to see along with air to breath."

Kaitleen looked at the people in her audience, who were definitely paying attention to her, so she launched into details. "The cerebral cortex, which is the outer layer of advanced brains, plays a key role in memory, attention, perception, awareness, thought, language, and consciousness. All animals have this to some degree, but in primates and cetaceans it's extremely well-developed. In determining how developed a brain is, scientists consider the brain's "encephalization" to be a significant factor. Since encephalization – the sinuous folds on the brain's surface – increases the amount of surface area for the cerebral cortex. Thus, the amount of encephalization is, in turn, considered an important factor and is only present in primate and cetacean brains. In fact, cetacean brains have even more encephalization than human brains, with the dolphin brain having 40 percent more cerebral cortex than a human. They apparently need this extra to handle the sea environment in which they live."

A well-dressed man in a suit and tie raised his hand. "Another characteristic of intelligence is that humans use tools when they work. Of course, we have hands and we work together in groups. Is there anything similar to that with dolphins?"

"Yes," answered Kaitleen, "in the wild, dolphins have been observed using sponges to protect their noses while foraging food, and they have also been known to use sticks to herd fish. Dolphins have also been observed carrying rocks in their mouths and then using them to dig in the sand for food or to crack open shells. That shows dolphins are capable of recognizing objects as tools and using them to accomplish a specific task. They're also capable of working together to solve problems, which suggests that they also have a high level of social intelligence."

There were no more immediate questions and thus Kaitleen led the group past the large tank toward a smaller one that was open to the outside and where there was seating for humans. "Dolphins live in groups called pods and communicate vocally through whistles, clicks, and pulsed sounds. Just as humans can be identified by speech, each dolphin has its own whistle. Our research indicates that dolphins are capable of using syntax and grammar in their vocalizations. It appears that they can combine different sounds to create new meanings and convey complex information."

“I thought the sounds they emitted help them navigate,” said a lady walking next to Kaitleen.

“That’s true also,” responded a delighted Kaitleen who was enjoying this group and continued to add more to her talk because more people int the group were asking questions, “it’s called echolocation, and it’s a process in which the dolphin emits high-frequency clicks and listens for the echoes that bounce back off objects. By analyzing these echoes, the dolphin can determine the location, size, and shape of objects in its environment. They also use echolocation to communicate with each other by emitting clicks and listening for the clicks of their pod members. It’s also clear that each dolphin has its own unique whistle, which it uses to identify itself, even if they’re not in close proximity to other dolphins. They also use a variety of gestures, such as head nods and tail slaps to convey messages. It’s these vocalizations and echolocation abilities along with their highly social behavior and interactions that are complex and varied that show they form strong bonds with one another and which document their intelligence.”

By this time the group had climbed stairs and moved outside where there was a viewing stand over a large outdoor pool. “I’ve seen their synchronized swimming, jumping, and other behaviors,” noted the man who had been skeptical before.

“Yes,” said Kaitleen, “and there will be a dolphin show at this pool at 3 pm. Let me just add that researchers have also observed dolphins having structured discussions with one another. It shows they are able to communicate with other dolphins in a highly organized and complex manner using whistles, clicks, and pulsed sounds.”

"You've made a strong case for them to be ranked right behind humans in intelligence," said Parker, "because they're able to learn and then communicate."

"Yes, and I believe they have long-term memory capabilities. The dolphins that observed you next to me at the aquarium would now recognize you if we walked back to them," responded Kaitleen.

"Is there a way of measuring intelligence among the many diverse forms of life?" asked Parker.

"One measure is to take account of the size of the brain relative to the animal's body size. By that measure dolphins are second only to humans, indicating that they have a high level of cognitive ability," replied Kaitleen. By this time the group had walked past the pool and were about to exit the entire Dolphinarium.

She concluded: "Dolphins have a high density of neurons in their cerebral cortex, which is the part of the brain responsible for cognitive processing. They have more neurons in this area than humans, which suggests that they have the potential for complex cognitive abilities. There's no standardized IQ test for dolphins or any test that can be applied across all animals. Considering the great diversity of life across the planet and given that intelligence is a complex concept that is difficult to measure, it's not possible to determine which animal is smarter as intelligence is highly specialized for their respective environments. Anyway, that ends our tour and thank you for showing an interest in dolphins."

With that, the group broke into applause, and a collective thank you to Kaitleen for an instructive view of dolphins. As the Spooner family separated from the group, Grace looked at her father and said, “If these mammals are that intelligent, I wonder if humans should be keeping them in zoos. I would think that we would be trying to communicate with them in the oceans.”

“Unfortunately, they don’t have hands so they can’t play chess,” said Peter, looking at his older sister.

“They would do it mentally and convey their moves by whistles, but we would have to learn their language,” replied a thoughtful Grace.

Parker smiled. Grace was a perceptive person, indicating the need to understand the dolphin language. Parker thought it was likely that research was already happening and that humans were already trying to communicate with the dolphins that roamed freely in the oceans.

When they arrived home, Rosemary removed a note that she had pinned to a message board above the telephone which rested on a stand between the kitchen and dining room. “You had a telephone call from Miss Qundo. She wants to talk to you but would not tell me what she was calling about and said she has already left a similar message on your office phone. She then gave me her Florida phone number. She also said small apple and please have Parker call me today even if it’s late. Then surprising me, she said she wanted to talk to me and so we did.”

“Really, what did you talk about?” asked Parker.

“We’ll talk about it tonight, darling. Right now, Miss Qundo is likely anxiously waiting by her phone for your call.”

Rosemary and Parker exchanged smiles as Parker sat down next to the telephone and Rosemary went into the kitchen. Parker looked at Oscar's latest black book that had recently arrived in his mail and was now next to the phone with an unsigned printed note, 'Oscar said <u>not</u> to give this book to the corrupt police.' Parker took this message seriously and had not shared the new black book or its message with anyone, including his father-in-law.

The last entry in the black book was 5/31 $10k w. Parker read this to mean that Oscar had withdrawn $10,000 and had that money when the killer arrived. LOOK TO COLLECT ALL MONEY BY ELEVEN was how the note read. Oscar had complied – he had the money - and yet he had been murdered. Perhaps Oscar was buying information for the purpose of revealing a spy. Yet the buyer must have been suspicious of Oscar and thus killed him. Parker speculated further that Oscar, in turn, probably recognized he was in danger with a late-night meeting and thus had already given his black book to someone who then mailed it to Parker. This black book was similar to the prior one found in the furnace and had the names of dozens of individuals who had placed bets with Oscar, but nothing immediately stood out other than the word, anagram, that had been written by Oscar on the back cover. Parker pondered this, but at this moment, he had to call Aurelia Qundo. He dialed her number and when she answered, he said, "Small apple. It's Parker Spooner, and I understand from my wife that you called me earlier today."

"Yes, and small apple to you. I want to discuss Oscar's murder with you. We're constructing dossiers discussing two different individuals. Either one could be the likely killer of Oscar, and we would like you to review the reports when they're finished. Our target date for completion is Wednesday, July 12. We don't want to put this information in the mail. Would you be willing to fly to our Miami office at our expense to review the dossiers and have us talk with you when they're finished?"

"Miami would be difficult for me since my family is going to be at Disney World that week. My daughter just graduated from high school, and we're going to be driving down there to celebrate with the family. We'll be in Orlando that entire week in July," said Parker.

"Okay," responded Miss Qundo, "Orlando as a site will work for me, but I don't know about Frank. Please hang on a moment while I check." Parker heard a click and then some music – it was Don McLean singing American Pie. Parker smiled and sat back to enjoy the involved lyrics, which ran on for several minutes; however, rather quickly there was a second click, interrupting the song, and Aurelia was back on the phone talking, "Yes, Orlando works for Frank Jenkins and me. We're happy to drive up to Orlando from Miami and meet you near Disney World. We have an Orlando office next to Disney that we use. Our meeting with you might take as long as two hours. The other proviso that we have is that you can't mention this meeting to the Chicago police, nor your father-in-law nor your family nor anyone. After this initial meeting and your feedback, we will talk to the Chicago police and others at an appropriate time. Do I have your word that you will keep this initial meeting in Orlando a secret?"

"Yes, I can do that if that's your request."

"That's Frank Jenkins's request – to keep this meeting secret for the time being. He says your profile is a straight shooter and if you give me your word that you won't talk to anybody and that includes your wife and father-in-law, then you won't talk to anybody about this meeting."

Parker smiled and thought to himself 'My profile? Wow, the CIA has a dossier on me!' and then said out loud, "You have my word, I won't talk to anybody."

"Thank you, I'll be calling you later to verify the date and time for the meeting along with the directions to our Orlando office. As of now, the meeting will take place from 3 pm to 5 pm, on Wednesday July 12 at CIA's Orlando office. Goodbye." And with that, Miss Qundo hung up the phone. She was so quick; Parker wondered if Miss Qundo heard his goodbye.

Parker hung up the phone, and Rosemary came over to inquire of Parker about what had happened with his call. Parker merely shook his head and weakly smiled at her saying, "All is well."

Rosemary returned the smile with a nod. She knew her husband was a straight shooter.

(17) Pillow Talk

Rosemary, who was sitting in bed, had finished her evening prayers and turned to her husband, Parker. He was next to her and looking again at Oscar's last black book. He wondered about the anonymous source with the printed note, 'Oscar said <u>not</u> to give this book to the corrupt police.' This book also had the word ANAGRAM printed in capital letters on the back of the book. He had not figured out what all that meant and placed the black book on the night table next to his bed. "How did your monthly luncheon with your lady friends go today, darling."

"Very well but there was really nothing new with them. My big news was talking about you with that CIA woman, Aurelia. However, before I get into all that, I hear you had a busy day at the Zoo with the three kids. Anna couldn't stop talking about the dolphins, especially a small one that she named "Happy". Apparently Happy did a double flip after going through a hoop and then returned for a repeated performance. Peter, instead of running to his chess board, went to the encyclopedia and has been reading about dolphins and other cetaceans. Even Grace, who is normally quiet when it comes to science, said she was surprised about what she learned at the Brookfield Zoo. She wonders if we should keep intelligent mammals like dolphins in zoos."

"Yes," responded Parker, "the tour guide, Kaitleen, was outstanding and that prompted audience participation. There were many questions, and she made a case for dolphins being more advanced brain wise than apes. I learned several new things."

"Really, give me an example."

“I thought echolocation was interesting. Dolphins emit sounds which echo back to them showing them how to navigate.”

Rosemary laughed. “We could use that technology in cars. It could prevent a lot of accidents.”

“Yes, self-driving cars should happen sometime in the foreseeable future but tell me about your phone discussion with Miss Qundo.”

“Yes, it was interesting, and she wanted to verify a few things. She had my full name, the names of our children, your mother’s name, address, phone; and then the same info for my parents and, of course, she’s aware that my Dad is a Chicago police detective. Then she asked about where we live, and how we live – she’s aware of our two cars, my station wagon and your Buick. Then phone numbers, home, and your office. All of that information on us was correct. She then said that if you ever went missing for any length of time, I was to contact them immediately. She gave me a special phone number that’s monitored continuously. I already had that since you gave it to me, and I confirmed that with her.”

Parker said, “That’s good.”

“Then she gave me a secret word that I was to use if I was ever in trouble. Just work it into the conversation when I call. I’m not supposed to share it with anybody including you.”

Parker said, “Okay, that’s good.”

"If something strange happens to you – if you're not acting right or there's a change in your behavior, I'll let them know."

Parker said, "Yes, that's good."

Rosemary gave a deep sigh, "I'm not certain about that. This cloak and dagger stuff bothers me."

"Yes, it also bothers me, but it's a definite indication that we're in a cold war with the Soviet Union."

Rosemary reflected, "The Soviets are too aggressive. I remember their invasion of Czechoslovakia in 1968 because they thought Dubcek was too independent and leaning westward."

"Yes," said Parker, "They were worried about politics and their invasion was terrible. The Czech nation borders Austria and Germany. It's a European nation as is Germany. The Soviet empire stretches to the East, but East Berlin was carved out for them because of World War II. That was back then, and today the reality is that one of these days the Berlin Wall will come down."

"And now because of this cold war, you've got a murder to solve that involves a Soviet spy who likely killed a CIA agent," said Rosemary.

"Yes, Oscar's murder was likely political and certainly terrible."

And with that Parker and Rosemary gave each other a kiss and tried to go to sleep. But neither one could sleep, and they wound up in each other's arms.

(18) Father Joseph Says a Special Prayer

Father Joseph spent hours in prayer every day. He was amazed with the natural world and saw the effects of God's creative work in nature. In particular, on this day, he reflected on a prayer attributed to St. Francis of Assisi which went under the title Canticle of the Sun or the Canticle of Creation or the Canticle of the Creatures. He thought of this prayer because he spoke with Grace Spooner, who had recently graduated high school and then went to the Brookfield Zoo with her father and siblings and saw many of God's creatures. After Sunday mass at the church brunch, Grace related her experiences at the Zoo to interested fellow parishioners and Father Joseph. Thus, that evening, Father Joseph closed his eyes and thought about St. Francis of Assisi and recalled St. Francis's Canticle prayer. He also recalled the experiences Grace had expressed as she saw the dolphins at the Brookfield Zoo. All of this led Father Joseph to pray the Canticle that Sunday evening:

"O Most High, all-powerful, good Lord God, to you belong praise, glory, honor and all blessing.

Be praised, my Lord, for all your creation and especially for our Brother Sun, who brings us the day and the light; he is strong and shines magnificently. O Lord, we think of you when we look at him.

Be praised, my Lord, for Sister Moon, and for the stars which you have set shining and lovely
in the heavens.

Be praised, my Lord, for our Brothers Wind and Air and every kind of weather by which you, Lord, uphold life in all your creatures.

Be praised, my Lord, for Sister Water, who is very useful to us, humble and precious and pure. O Lord, and your seas are full of life in all your creatures.

Be praised, my Lord, for Brother Fire, through whom you give us light in the darkness: he is bright and lively and strong.

Be praised, my Lord, for Sister Earth, our Mother, who nourishes us and sustains us, bringing forth fruits and vegetables of many kinds and flowers of many colors.

Be praised, my Lord, for those who forgive for the love of you; and for those who bear sickness and weakness in peace and patience - you will grant them a crown.

Be praised, my Lord, for our Sister Death, whom we must all face. I praise and bless you, Lord,
and I give thanks to you, and I will serve you in all humility. Amen."

With that Father Joseph became silent and meditated on the Glory of God experienced in nature. He recalled that St. Clare of Assisi became one St. Francis's followers and made a mental note to study her contribution to the church as her feast day approached in August.

(19) Susan in Miami

Susan Danford was back at the same Miami resort where she and Oscar had stayed in April. This time she was by herself and kept a low profile for the first two days of her visit. She quietly checked out the staff both inside the building and the men who handled the cars and transportation on the outside. She recognized the faces of four staff on the inside and two of the men who handled the outside transportation. She discreetly approached one of car attendants and asked him about Boris Volkov who had a Russian accent and had parked his car in the lot when he visited the hotel last April. The attendant didn't remember any such person. She had more success with the second attendant who remembered Boris but didn't know his last name. She had a slightly different but similar reaction when she mentioned a golden hair woman driving a white Mercedes. Both attendants remembered the lady with the car but didn't know her name and neither attendant had seen either Boris or Golden Hair since last April.

Susan also had no luck with the waiters in the main restaurant, who didn't remember either Boris or the golden-haired woman. Since neither one had checked into the resort but had only visited the place to see Oscar, the main resort desk was not able to help Susan. However, Susan finally had success when she stopped for a drink at the bar and mentioned Boris by his first name. The bartender was of Russian decent and remembered talking to a Boris Volkov, a fellow Russian, one afternoon last April while the guy waited for his friend. When the friend showed up, the two left the resort in Boris's car, but the bartender and Boris had talked, and Boris bragged that he owned a large boat and frequently went out on the ocean. Susan asked the name of the boat or where it was docked but the barkeeper didn't know. Nevertheless, Susan said a quiet prayer of thanks that she had stopped at the bar and found a bartender who remembered Boris. She was on her way to track him down.

Susan next task was to check out all the piers that housed private boats. North Miami seemed to be a place loaded with such piers, and so she started her search for Boris in North Miami. She remembered what Boris looked like, and she also remembered what the golden hair woman looked like, but for the moment she put finding the woman out of mind and concentrated on finding Boris Volkov. There were dozens of boats docked in North Miami and methodically Susan walked the piers asking strangers for a man named Boris who had a Russian accent. Very soon she was directed four piers north to a boat named *1922,* which Boris owned and now for the first time Susan became worried as she stood next to the empty docked boat. Susan knew 1922 was the year the Bolsheviks came to power in Russia, and Boris was brazened enough to name his boat to honor the year that event took place. Oscar had been murdered, and Susan felt Boris had something to do with the murder, having seen him last April in Miami, but now it dawned on her that the Cold War between the United States and the Soviet Union might be the larger story behind Oscar's murder. She would retreat to her hotel to rethink a possible encounter with Boris. And she also wondered about the golden-haired woman in a Mercedes.

(20) Susan Talks to Parker

The next two days, Susan carefully followed Boris and observed his activities. She then decided she needed help and the only person she could think of was Parker. She had mailed him Oscar's black book, and he was involved in solving Oscar's murder, so the information she had would be of value to him. She went to a phone booth dialed his office number one morning early and was happy to hear, "Good morning, this is Parker Spooner, how may I help you?"

"Good morning, Parker, this is Susan Delford. I'm calling you from a phone booth in Miami, Florida. I've got quite-a-bit of information and hope you have time to talk."

"I'm surprised and happy to hear from you, Susan. My father-in-law, Sergeant Michael Boyle of the Chicago Police Department has been trying to locate you for weeks."

"I'm not hiding but keeping very much to myself and let me start by saying that I was in Oscar's apartment the night he was murdered. He had telephoned me that day and said it was important that I should come to his apartment that night. I went, and he gave me his black book. He said it contained important information and that if something happened to him to give it the book to Bob Hanson. Under no circumstances was I to give the book to the police because there was corruption there. When your father-in-law interviewed me after the murder, I lied about not being in Oscar's apartment and kept the book a secret because of what Oscar told me about corrupt police."

"Okay, but then you mailed the book to me without identifying yourself but with a note to keep it from the police. I've done that – the police haven't seen it. There's nothing different about this black book from an earlier one that both I and the police have seen except the word ANAGRAM is printed on the back of this book, and I'm not certain how that word applies to Oscar's murder. Do you know anything about this at all?"

"No, I don't. After Oscar's death I looked for Bob Hanson to give him the book as I promised Oscar, but Bob wasn't around. Moreover, he didn't attend Oscar's Funeral, and then I learned that Bob had inherited money and was off to Iceland to view the World Chess Championship. That made no sense to me. I thought the story might be fake, and I panicked worried about spies being involved and mailed the book to you because you aren't a policeman."

"I have the book but haven't made much sense of it nor have I shared it with anyone. You just said you panicked about spies. What's that about?" inquired Parker.

Susan took a deep breath and launched into an explanation that had a surprise for Parker, "Last April Oscar and I went to Miami and there I saw he was involved with strange people. There was a man Boris Volkov with a Russian accent and a beautiful blond woman driving a white Mercedes. The night of the murder - Oscar told me *he was worried about spies and the black book he was giving me.* I believe he was killed for that book and now I had it. I got rid of it by mailing it to you and then I left Chicago for Miami and have been laying low but investigating. I don't know who the woman with the white Mercedes is but I've located Boris. I know where he lives and what he's been doing." Parker noted the beautiful blond woman driving a white Mercedes had to be Aurelia Qundo, but he didn't say that to Susan.

"Susan, please be careful. It may be prudent for you to leave the area. If you are watching Boris, whoever he is, then you've probably been noticed. Is there some place you could go at least temporarily?"

"I have a college friend who lives in Fort Lauderdale – I could see if she's around."

"That's a good idea. Give your friend a call and see if you can connect with her. If you do and are staying there, then call me with your address and phone number. Before you go, let me ask about Boris Volkov and then the woman driving a Mercedes. You said you know what Boris is currently doing. Can you describe exactly what that is?"

"He has a large cabin cruiser and goes out on the ocean. He carries a tape recorder and is gone for hours. When he returns, he carries the tape recorder into his apartment and disappears for the rest of the day. Then the next day he repeated the same thing – out to the ocean with his recorder and then he returns to his apartment. This morning he carried a package to the local post office. I don't know if he mails it or leaves it in a box for someone else to pick it up, but that's what he has been doing. After the post office, Boris went out on the ocean in his boat again. To me it seems that he was meeting someone out on the ocean and recording their conversation. Then coming home and mailing it to someone else."

"Is his apartment close to the dock?"

"Yes, very close – almost directly across the street from the dock."

"Is the place busy – are there many people around as he comes and goes?"

"Yes, these docks are busy all day – people walking back and forth all the time."

"All right – so he may not have spotted you yet. That's good. Now what about the woman that you spotted last April? How's she related to Boris and Oscar?"

"During my April trip, I never saw her with Boris, but the night I followed Oscar, he met this woman at a café, and she and Oscar talked at some length. She's young enough to be his daughter, but the blonde golden hair and her facial features are very different from Oscar, so I don't think they're related. Also, they didn't act like former lovers, so I think this was some form of business meeting, but when I mentioned golden hair to Oscar, he refused to talk about her or their relationship. I don't know her name. Nevertheless, seeing both Boris and this woman last April, I knew Oscar was involved in something that I wanted to avoid. But now with Oscar's death, I want the people who killed him identified and behind bars, whether they're spies or not." Susan took a long pause and when Parker didn't respond, she asked, "Do you know who Boris Volkov is and how he's related to the golden hair woman and their relationship to Oscar?"

"You have really done a good piece of detective work, Miss Danford, and yes, I know these people. I'm aware of Boris, Oscar, and the woman you described. Your description of Boris's trips out on the ocean are invaluable. I'll be passing this along – please go under cover in Fort Lauderdale at your friend's house."

After saying goodbye to Susan, Parker immediately telephoned Aurelia Qundo. He briefly described what Susan had mentioned about Boris Volkov's boat trips into the Atlantic Ocean. Aurelia responded that the CIA was aware of Boris and another person, and their movements were being closely monitored. She was happy that Susan was now removing herself from potential danger by going to Fort Lauderdale away from the docks and ocean where all of this was playing out.

The call ended and Aurelia was surprised that Parker, who the agency wanted to hire to investigate Oscar's murder, was now involved in another aspect of CIA work, and this one involved a closely guarded secret that was taking place in the ocean off the Florida coast. Meanwhile, Parker, once the call ended, wondered what was going on in the ocean off the Miami Fort Lauderdale coastline.

Susan, meanwhile, after leaving the phone booth, was surrounded by the Florida police. They had a warrant for her arrest from the Chicago police department, and she was to be extradited back to Chicago for questioning regarding the murder of Oscar Busby. Susan remained calm and fully cooperated with the police. She would return and be questioned by the Chicago police as to what she was doing in Oscar's apartment the night he was murdered. She would hire a lawyer, inform Parker as to what was happening, and say nothing to the corrupt Chicago police.

(21) Dmitri Doby

Dmitry Doby was a young man who earned his master's degree in marine biology from Auburn University in 1967 and had plans to continue studying marine mammals such as whales and dolphins that belonged to the biological order named Cetacea. He was also interested in civil rights and in the 1960's he often protested at restaurants that were not allowing all Americans to eat in their establishments. To a large extent his political views were shaped by his father and grandfather, both of whom were quiet card-carrying communists, but they were not involved in the operations of the party even before 1954 when the Communist Party was made illegal in the United States. At first, Dmitry did not join the party or express such views, in part because he wasn't that interested and also because he was looking for research money to further his knowledge of sea mammals.

Dmitri was the only child of Igor and Claira Doby, born in Chicago as World War II was ending. He was a quiet and sensitive child and as such was bothered when he observed bad things happening to those around him. In spite of his very protective mother, Dmitri noticed many different bad things happening to various people. His playmates and friends would join gangs and get into street fights, or they would cheat on school tests. He managed to avoid most of this and developed a strong sense that he always wanted to do the right thing. Once when he was 12 years old, his mother gave him money to buy himself an ice cream cone from the Good Humor truck that came through the streets. Having purchased a double scoop of chocolate ice cream, but before he started licking it, Dmitri noticed a young girl crying next to her mother. Both were dressed in shabby clothes. The mother had just told her daughter that she did not have enough money to buy the girl an ice cream cone, and Dmitri, without hesitation, handed the girl his ice cream cone, “Here little girl, this is for you,” he said smiling at her.

The little girl immediately hugged Dmitri’s leg looking up to him with tears still in her eyes but now with a big smiling face, “Oh, thank you, thank you, kind sir!” she cried. Dmitry thought the girl was beautiful by her actions and gently pulled away from her. The mother was now also loudly thanking Dmitry, who was embarrassed and could only nod to the woman. Other individuals near the ice cream truck were now noticing him. He did not know what to say or do, and thus, he ran away. Dmitry certainly did not want people looking at him or praising him for doing something that was correct. He thought that doing the right thing was the only way to live and was both surprised and embarrassed if someone praised him for that action.

As he grew older, he went to a large public high school and made the school’s basketball team. He was never a starter, but a reliable backup when the star players got into trouble. He could control the ball and move it down the court, but his shooting ability was below average, which was why he never started. He fell in love associating with two of the girl cheer leaders, but they already had boyfriends and rather than trying to compete, Dmitry just kept his head down and made no further attempt to attract their attention. Dmitry thought he did the right thing. If the girls really liked him, they would have told him.

In college, he spent most of the time studying and doing well academically at Auburn University where he had earned a full-time scholarship majoring in biological studies. He dated infrequently, finding most of the woman that attracted him physically beautiful but mentally shallow. Most of the time, he stayed quiet and by himself. Finally, it was United States involvement in the ongoing Vietnam War that became the major factor which drove Dmitry to become publicly vocal. He was distressed that young American men were dying in a war that shouldn't have involved the United States. Throughout the mid 1960's Dmitri became increasing active in protests against the United States involvement in that war because to him such involvement was clearly wrong – it wasn't right to have American men dying in Southeast Asia! Thus, in mid-October 1967, Dmitri was part of the 100,000 war protesters who gathered in Washington, DC. They conducted a peaceful rally at the Lincoln Memorial, but then about a third of the group, including Dmitry, marched to the Pentagon. There soldiers from the 82nd Airborne Division blocked the Pentagon steps and prevented access to the building. Many protesters led by Abbie Hoffman and Allen Ginsberg performed silly but peaceful symbolic acts such as calling on 'psychic energy' to levitate the Pentagon building.

As that day wore on some of the protests escalated into a confrontation between demonstrators and military personnel. A handful of protesters attempted to enter the Pentagon but were repelled by soldiers using tear gas and physical force. A faceoff between protesters and troops with bayonets lasted for hours and finally around midnight the soldiers chased most of the protesters away. Afterwards, there were 47 reported injuries among protesters, soldiers, and U.S. Marshalls and arrests numbered around 680, according to official reports.

Dmitry witnessed most of this. He was neither arrested nor injured that night but highly critical of how the Government handled the Pentagon demonstration. Very soon thereafter, he joined the illegal American Communist Party and when his father and grandfather called for a quiet meeting to induct their son/grandson into the Party, Dmitry spoke to the group about the Pentagon incident that he had witnessed, "It was totally mishandled by Robert McNamara who watched the start of a peaceful demonstration from the Pentagon rooftop and allowed it to develop over hours into a warlike situation. McNamara should have called for the protesters to form a small group of serious, thoughtful protesters, excluding all the media clowns, and invited this small group into the Pentagon for a meaningful conversation. Then there would have been no storming of the building, no injuries, no arrests, and finally the nation would have been on its way to a constructive end of the illegal and horrible Vietnam war." The small group of men in the crowded apartment kept applauding Dmitry. He stood there, beaming at hearing the ongoing applause. Dmitry had been noticed and was no longer embarrassed by doing something right.

Very soon after joining the Party, Dmitry met Sergei Kotov who was fluent in English and Russian and frequently traveled between America and Europe. Sergei had heard about Dmitry joining the Party and wanted to meet him. The two started talking, and Sergei immediately recognized Dmitry as an idealist and naïve about politics. Sergei set about recruiting Dmitry to gather information that would help the Soviet Union in its struggle against capitalism. As the United States became entrenched in Vietnam, Dmitry became more distressed with America's involvement and then went beyond anything his parents had ever done, and finally, because of Sergei's persuasion, Dmitry agreed to gather sensitive information or to spy for the Soviet Union.

At this moment, when he committed to spying, Dmitry had no real knowledge as to what spying entailed, but he was completely convinced that this was the proper and the correct pathway to take, and he even told Sergei that he was willing to take on "difficult" assignments as long as they didn't physically harm anyone he had to deal with directly. Dmitry said that he just wanted to do the right thing in all circumstances.

Sergei wasn't certain about the idealist, Dmitry Doby, but Sergei did have something happening in Chicago, which was Dmitry's hometown and for which Dmitry was perfectly suited. Thus, Sergei asked Dmitry to temporarily move back to Chicago using funds that would be given to him and make the acquaintance of Edward Murray who was working at Argonne National Laboratory in an area that was developing an electronic device that would study sea mammals. Sergei said Dmitry's first assignment was to meet Edward and then obtain as much information as possible of Edward's plans for the device. Dmitry's background in marine biology would be invaluable in approaching Edward and starting a conversation. Dmitry was to pass along whatever information he could get out of Edward to Sergei. Comrades in Russia were also working on a similar device and having problems so that even partial or incomplete data could be helpful to them.

Thus, a few weeks later, Dmitry was living in Chicago and visited O'Rourke's, a tavern on North Avenue, that was a local hangout for many famous Chicagoans including Roger Ebert, movie critic for the *Chicago Sun Times* and many actors from the nearby Second City Revue. At O'Rourke's on any given night, you might see Mike Royko, Studs Terkel, John Belushi, or Jay Robert Nash, a prolific crime writer along with Al the Greek and sometimes press agents would bring in visiting movie stars. Many of the folks in the bar became fake Irishmen because of the Clancy Brothers music that played at O'Rourke's and large blown-up photographs of Brendan Behan, Sean O'Casey, (George) Bernard Shaw, and James Joyce.

It was known that Edward spent his weekends drinking and socializing there along with many other folks, some of them looking for breakout opportunities in theater, movies, or TV. Many of the others merely felt comfortable in this environment, which was the case for Edward Murray. Dmitry circulated talking to various people but stayed close to Edward who was seated at the bar. Eventually a spot next to Edward opened, and Dmitry slid in and extended his hand to Edward, introducing himself and soon the two men were chatting. Edward was quiet about his work but indicated he was a UC graduate with a physics degree.

Dmitry, in turn, lied and said he was new to the city of Chicago and continued, "I'm helping out at the Brookfield Zoo working as a marine biologist. They have a wonderful Dolphinarium, and we're trying to learn more about these amazing mammals." He noticed that Edward looked surprised, and thus to avoid suspicion, Dmitry immediately shifted attention away from dolphins by saying, "You know this tavern is also amazing, and seems to have a well-educated clientele. None of these folks are really hippies but it certainly seems different from mainstream Chicago once you listen to some of them talk."

"A lot of single people here," said Edward, "and yes, if you listen to them talk and get into some serious subjects with them, you might understand why many of them remain single."

Dmitry smiled. He didn't understand the real meaning of Edward's drift but sensed that Edward might be half drunk. Dmitry had asked Sergei for information about the device that both the Soviets and the Americans at Argonne were attempting to build. As such, Dmitry had been given drawings and a written description of a recording device.

He studied the Soviet material and wanted to probe Edward but decided to wait and not immediately start questioning him. If Dmitry was careful with his questions and Edward got drunk enough and thought of Dmitry as a friend, then he might eventually learn something significant about the recording device. Thus, that first meeting between Edward and Dmitry lasted another hour of idle friendly chatter before Dmitry excused himself, "I'll be back next Friday night, Edward. I hope to see you then."

"Take care, Dmitry. Next week I would like to learn about your work with dolphins at the zoo," responded Edward. Dmitry smiled. He had succeeded with Edward in their first meeting. Edward was comfortable with his new friend and next time Dmitry would describe a tour that he took of the Brooklyn Zoo Dolphinarium along with the dolphin show, which would then allow him to segway into asking Edward critical questions about the development of the electronic device.

Thus, the following week the two men discussed the tricks that the dolphins did during the show at Brookfield and eventually the conversation drifted into the possibility of communicating with the species. "I don't think that will be possible," said Dmitry, "There are two kinds of ideas: perceptual ideas and conceptual ideas. Perceptual ideas are tied to an image or a perception – the person has a 'picture thought'. These are the kinds of ideas that are common to humans and also to some species of animals such as apes and dolphins. Thus, an image of a hoop and a dolphin jumping through the hoop can be conveyed from humans to a dolphin. Conceptual ideas are those arising out of a relationship among ideas both conceptual and perceptual. Conceptual ideas may be tied to perceptual ideas, but they go beyond those ideas by setting them into a relationship with each other, which is only done by humans."

"So, you don't think it's possible for another species besides us humans to communicate intelligibility," said Edward.

"Wouldn't we have found that out already? Look at how long humans have been trying to communicate with apes," responded Dmitry, "Apes can pick out objects, which is perception, but cannot distinguish between 'Dog bites Man' and 'Man bites Dog'.

"Yes, but we know little about how whales, dolphins, and other cetaceans communicate underwater where it's dark," said Edward.

"Okay, that's true, but the Brookfield Zoo has been doing all sorts of work in trying to understand dolphins," responded Dmitry. Edward merely smiled and didn't say anything. Dmitry thought that was enough for one night and changed the subject.

A week later Dmitry was back at O'Rourke's and showed Edward several diagrams. He had copied some of the work that the Soviets had done and claimed that he obtained the diagrams on several pieces of paper by talking to biologists visiting the Brookfield Zoo. The papers showed various markings that represented various sounds that dolphins emitted. Their whistles and clicks had been translated into English and crude English sentences were displayed. Edward really took notice of these pieces of paper and asked if he could borrow them. Dmitry agreed, and thus another night and week passed at O'Rourke's tavern where patrons sang, talked, played darts and generally enjoyed themselves in conversations. Edward now had some of the Soviets' work on the development of the electronic device, and Dmitry spent an anxious week waiting for the next Friday session.

Edward was there and greeted Dmitry warmly. There was a big discussion among O'Rourke's regulars opining on the best American war movie. 'The Bridge on the Rive Kwai' Columbia Pictures 1957 seemed to be the winner. After that discussion Edward started discussing foreign war films with Dmitry, who didn't say much because he didn't know anything about foreign films and was waiting for Edward to bring up the dolphin documents from the prior week. On this particular night, the tavern was as loud as possible, and Edward was drinking more than normal. Dmitry bided his time, waiting for Edward to broach the topic that the two had discussed the prior week. More time passed, and Edward finally brought out the diagrams that Dmitry had given him the prior week. Edward looked apprehensive and then said, "None of the work done by your biologist friends at the Brookfield Zoo made any sense. I took the opportunity to revise them," and with that he handed the papers back to Dmitry.

"I don't think I understand any of this," replied Dmitry looking at the marked-up diagrams, "but I'll give them to the guys at Brookfield." The rest of the night and early morning passed before Dmitry exited the tavern. "See you next week," said Edward.

However, the following Friday, Dmitry did not show. Edward sat there and became worried. He realized he didn't have Dmitry's phone number or address. *He's probably not feeling well* was Edward's thought; however, when Dmitry didn't show the next Friday, Edward called the Brookfield Zoo and found out that no one at the zoo knew Dmitry nor the biologists that Dmitry said had given him the diagrams.

Edward realized that he had been tricked and had provided classified information when he commented on Dmitry's diagrams, changing them so that the device represented would now work if physically constructed. Like so many lonely men Edward had passed sensitive information to a friendly stranger.

Edward's classified project at Argonne National Laboratory was titled, "An electronic translator of cetacean sounds." This was not a highly classified project, but nevertheless, it was classified. They were developing a machine that would help translate dolphin sounds into English with the hope that the sea mammals were more intelligent than apes and that the two species could begin communicating. Clearly, if humans and cetaceans could ever communicate with each other on conceptual ideas, that would be earth shaking.

Dmitry reflected on what he had accomplished, and it now bothered him. He had helped his comrades, but he had deliberately lied and deceived Edward, and this tempered Dmitry's entire attitude. He vowed never to do something wrong like that again. Sergei praised Dmitry's deceit, but Dmitry was not happy with himself or Sergei's praise. He began to dislike Sergei, who carried a gun and acted like a thug. This Soviet agent was a very different communist from the quiet sleeper cell that Dmitry knew as a child growing up with his father and grandfather. As Dmitri subsequently met other party members, he realized that they were all closer to Sergei than to his father and grandfather. Thus, Dmitri began to question Soviet actions throughout the world.

(22) Dmitry and Aurelia

As Dmitry was attending classes in marine biology at Auburn University, he noticed a beautiful golden-haired woman in many of his classes. Her name was Aurelia Qundo, and she was going to receive her M.S. in marine biology the same year as he would, 1967. By that time, they had become friendly and shared classroom information about cetaceans, especially dolphins. Both Aurelia and Dmitry immediately liked each other because they thought similarly about cetaceans and after graduation both wanted to pursue research on these sea dwelling mammals.

Because of her physical beauty many of the men in Aurelia's classes attempted to date her. Aurelia quickly made it clear to everyone that she wouldn't accept sexual advances, touching, kissing, or engage in sexual innuendos. She wore long pants or long skirts to hide her legs, and her breasts were always covered. She was there to study, and her long-range goal was to make advancements in marine biology. If you wanted to go out on the weekends, that was good and Aurelia would go with you once all her homework and research was done and if a useful lecture was available.

Dmitry had observed and heard all of this from the other men and initially stopped thinking about a romance with her. He was one of the few guys that never asked Aurelia for a date and thus never heard her quiet "No, thank you, I'm busy that night." Additionally, in Dmitry's mind there was another aspect about her background that precluded him from pursuing her. Aurelia's family came from Cuba, and they had to flee the island when the Castros came to power. Thus, Aurelia and her family rejected communism in any form. Strong political differences came to light during 1960's because of the turmoil occurring in the

United States over the Vietnam war. Both Dmitri and Aurelia recognized their background differences, which almost caused them to stop being friends. However, they avoided discussing the war and even politics and thus remained friends and collaborators as they studied cetaceans, the highly intelligent sea dwellers, which excited their human intellectual curiosity.

After graduation, Aurelia was hired by a local research laboratory where she also taught students about sea mammals, while Dmitry went off to work in Chicago. Of course, he said nothing to Aurelia about his recruitment as a Soviet spy or his first assignment to find information about "an electronic translator of cetacean sounds". He was in Chicago for that work only a few weeks and then returned to Auburn University to do research in marine biology. Thus, Aurelia and Dmitry started seeing each other at various lectures and programs related to cetacean studies. These sessions deepened their general understanding of sea life with an emphasis on dolphins. Their intellectual excitement about studying dolphins and sharing their understanding grew. They didn't think that attending lectures and meetings together was similar to going out on a date, but the two certainly enjoyed themselves and became fond of each other during these occasions.

Because of lingering guilt over his actions with Edward and then sensing Sergei's hostility to everything American, Dmitry's opinion of communism had changed, and once he tried to convey some of that to Aurelia. "I want you to know that even though I'm against American involvement in Vietnam and have praised certain social conditions in communism that it's still my hope that there will be peace and cooperation among nations."

"Yes, everyone says they want peace," responded Aurelia, "but when I think of communism in my family's homeland, I think of how dissent was shut down by Castro. He shut down opposition once he gained power. That's not the way to peace and cooperation."

Dmitry didn't expect this from Aurelia and didn't immediately respond. Aurelia certainly had no idea that he was acting as a spy for Russia. He recognized he would be getting into deep waters by continuing to talk with her about communism and thus quickly switched the topic back to dolphins, the only topic of mutual interest and the reason for their ongoing relationship.

Dmitry told Aurelia he was conducting his own investigations into dolphins by listening carefully to their squeals, and then when the two of them were together in a laboratory, he demonstrated what he was doing. There they both listened to taped dolphin squeals that Dmitry had recorded in the ocean east of Miami as the dolphins jumped into the air. As Aurelia listened to the recorded sounds of dolphins leaping in the ocean, she thought she picked up a distinct "conversation" that the cetaceans were having. Dmitry, playing around with the various dolphin clicks and whistles on the tape recorder came up with what he thought was a response to their squeals and recorded it. Aurelia listened to his tape and made some suggestions. Dmitry made a second tape, while retaining the original. Aurelia had more ideas on the order and length of the dolphin whistles relative to the dolphin clicks, and soon additional tapes emerged.

"This weekend, I'm going to drive to the coast, rent a boat, and go out into the ocean to look for dolphins and attempt to communicate with them using these new tapes. Do you want to go along and help me?" asked Dmitri. Aurelia was excited and nodded yes – the two had definitely bonded with their shared experience of developing a 'talking' dolphin tape.

Thus, the two spent most of the daylight hours that Saturday on a boat in the ocean trying to get the attention of dolphins by playing the various tapes. They were unsuccessful. Nothing happened other than the dolphins leapt and kept going, oblivious to the sounds coming from the tape recorder and Dmitry's attempt to contact them. On that day there certainly was no communication with the sea mammals. "Early attempts, but I'm going to keep working on this idea. How about you, Aurelia?" asked Dmitry, hoping for her help. Dmitry knew she was incredibly smart and wanted to work with her studying dolphins. The notion that she was a beautiful woman and something romantic might develop between them was now in his mind, and he started thinking about bringing that possibility into reality.

"I don't think tape recording dolphin sounds has much chance at success," said Aurelia answering his question on communicating with dolphins and indirectly answering his unsaid question about developing a personal relationship. She continued, "We're a land-based species, and they're a water-based species living in the oceans. Real communication will be difficult and involve more technology than a simple tape recorder so I'm going to pass, but I wish you the best in your research." And thus, a disappointed Dmitri shrugged his shoulders and the two friends stopped working together.

Shortly after this disappointment, Dmitry heard about a job opening in Miami from Sergei Kotov. Dmitry was qualified for this job, and the Party wanted him to take it. Dmitry realized he was very well suited for this job and even though he was leery of Sergei at this point in their relationship, he applied for the job and because of his marine biology knowledge was hired and began working for the United States Navy. His position was the training of dolphins and sea lions as teammates for American Sailors and Marines to help guard against various underwater threats. These projects took him frequently to Atlantic Ocean sites along Florida's east coast including Cape Kennedy where American rockets were launching astronauts on trips to the moon.

Aurelia was sad to see Dmitry go to Miami but happy for him that he had found this job. She herself had applied for a job in Miami and was waiting for an interview with the Central Intelligence Agency. At that time, she still had no idea that Dmitri was acting as a spy for Russia or who Sergei Kotov was.

(23) Aurelia

Frank Jenkins had to hire a new person because the CIA was now studying dolphins. When the CIA was created, its purpose was to create a clearinghouse for *foreign* policy intelligence and analysis, collecting, analyzing, evaluating, and disseminating foreign intelligence, and carrying out *covert* operations. The CIA had no law enforcement function and focused on intelligence gathering overseas, with only limited domestic involvement because sometimes it was necessary to arrest individuals.

The attempt to understand dolphins was considered to be foreign intelligence, and the creation of dolphin spies was a new project for the CIA, which began to dominate office work and other projects because the Soviets were simultaneously doing the same thing along the Florida seacoast. Jenkins goal was to identify the Soviet spies doing dolphin research in the United States, have them arrested, and establish his own dolphins in American waters.

Aurelia Qundo's resume was impressive to Frank and after a preliminary background check gave her a high rating, she was invited for an interview. Upon arrival, Frank immediately asked about her knowledge of cetaceans, and a long discussion followed. Aurelia described her interest and research of dolphins. She also told Frank the details of how she and Dmitry had unsuccessfully tried to communicate with the sea mammals using tapes of their cliques and whistles. Frank was surprised by what he had just learned but showed no emotion or changes in his facial expression. Nevertheless, it was this revelation that sealed the deal, and he knew he wanted to hire her. Frank paused and thought a few seconds about the process of bringing Miss Qundo into the Agency.

During the pause, Aurelia was wondering about Frank. She guessed correctly that he was about 15 years older than her and was completely on top of his job. It was clear to her that the CIA was Frank's life. She was not aware that before Frank joined the CIA, he had a girlfriend, Mary. However, Frank was always interested in organizations like the Central Intelligence Agency, which was created in 1947 with the signing of the National Security Act by President Harry S. Truman. In the end, Frank joined the CIA against Mary's wishes, and she left him. Frank, in turn, threw himself completely into CIA work and never looked back.

Frank told Aurelia that she could start working for the CIA immediately as a secretary in their Miami office. He said this secretarial role was merely a cover devised by him for the CIA's secret work with dolphins. He then briefly told her what she would be doing. Frank told her she could not tell any of her friends or family that she was working on a secret dolphin project but merely to say that she was a secretary at the CIA. Aurelia agreed to this and said she would not even mention her CIA position and allow others to believe that she was still working at a research lab and delivering lectures on cetaceans to various interested groups. Within a few minutes, Frank offered and Aurelia accepted her CIA assignment.

The hiring of Aurelia was an easy decision for Frank because of her background and knowledge of cetaceans and her obvious intelligence. The fact that she was a beautiful woman was not a factor in his initial evaluation of her. Within a short period of time, he became even more impressed with her work in the office and how she handled CIA business, and because it was impossible not to recognize both her intellectual and physical beauty, Frank began to think of her as a very special woman. He had no romantic notions or experiences with any women since Mary had departed from his life. Outwardly, Frank gave no evidence to Aurelia that she was someone special but wondered how long that could continue because he was falling in love with her and suspected that she might feel that way about him.

Within days of her hire, Aurelia was approved to work on the CIA dolphin project. This was a highly classified project within the CIA, and only Frank Jenkins and Aurelia knew about this work in the Miami office. The other agents - Stein, Watts, and Williams – suspected something special was happening but being CIA agents kept their noses out of it.

As Aurelia started working directly with Frank Jenkins, she soon found herself fantasizing about him as a man. He was 15 years older than her, but his razor-sharp mind and style were attractive to her, and under his sometimes abrupt actions, there was always a sense that he wanted to do the correct thing. Aurelia liked that trait in a man. "I wonder if he has a girlfriend or was ever married?" questioned Aurelia to herself. Quick research answered both of her questions with a definite "no" and with that Aurelia became a very happy worker for Frank Jenkins. Moreover, she soon found herself not only working very hard but with complete compatibly alongside Frank. She anticipated many of his next moves and had the folders and backup papers ready before he asked. He was aware of her foreknowledge and thanked her for her acuteness. Aurelia told herself to remain calm, but she couldn't deny that she had fallen in love with him.

Then she asked herself the important question, what did Frank think of her? In terms of competency and working together, there was no doubt he was pleased, and he expressed that in many ways. But was he attracted to her as a woman? It was clear to her that Frank was completely involved with running the Miami office of the CIA. She understood that, and the particular trait of being totally committed to his work was one reason that caused her to love him as a man; however, she wasn't certain of his feelings for her. She might have to wait and see how he felt about her as a woman, but as long as they worked together, it would eventually become clear how he felt even if the answer came at the end and was "Thank you, Miss Qundo, but it's time for you to move to another CIA office. All the best to you." Aurelia thought about that and decided that ending was unlikely. She knew that she was beautiful and smart, and that Frank was an exception man who privately recognized her beauty and appreciated her intelligence, and thus the two of them would eventually find each other.

(24) Dmitri's Fear

The new CIA project was learning how to communicate with dolphins. This was exactly what Dmitry and Aurelia attempted to do one weekend in the distant past when they went out on the ocean with a tape recorder and attempted to contact dolphins. As she started work in the CIA Miami office, Aurelia did not know that after their failed experiment, Dmitry on his own had successfully started communicating with dolphins. A slightly modified version of their prior attempt to communicate had produced success for Dmitry. Indeed, almost immediately after their failed ocean attempt, Dmitry, experimenting alone, found that if the taped dolphin whistles and clicks were made a touch louder, then the dolphins responded. If those whistles and clicks were too soft or too loud the dolphins ignored them but at exactly the correct sound frequency, the dolphins responded and a simple conversation had started, at least with some of the dolphins, who now recognized certain English words. Under the guidance of Sergei Kotov, Dmitry started working with Boris Volkov, and the two of them were recording dolphin voices and attempting conversations where information would be transmitted between the two species. A high level of conversation had not been accomplished, but what had happened was already revolutionary for Dmitry, and he thought he would go down in history if the work continued and more "words" were recorded and understood between the dolphins and humans.

Several months after she started working for the CIA, Aurelia found herself at a homecoming party for Auburn graduates, and Dmitry was there. The two friends greeted each other but during the course of the evening it became clear that Dmitry was troubled by her new job, which was a research secretary at the CIA. She had never mentioned the CIA to the homecoming committee having identified herself as a research secretary for various technical journals studying cetaceans. How did Dmitri know that she had taken a position at the CIA? Obviously, someone had told him. Yes, Dmitri was shocked and frightened when Sergei told him that Aurelia was now working for the CIA, and his face reflected that fear. However, when he spoke to Aurelia at the homecoming, he merely said to her that she was exceptionally bright, and he was surprised that she would settle for a secretary's position. Aurelia covered herself by saying that her CIA secretarial job involved reading many technical journals and summarizing them in detail, where a normal secretarial position wouldn't have all that technical reading.

Dmitry smiled and nodded, but he remained upset over her job. Aurelia was now part of the CIA, an organization that would put him in jail because he was spying for a foreign power. Aurelia, in turn, recalled that Dmitry was training dolphins and sea lions to protect the country from underwater threats, while her work at the CIA was doing almost the same thing but on a much broader scale and, of course, there was a classified piece to a portion of her work. Aurelia realized that Dmitry somehow knew about her new job at the CIA and that he was now worried. Very quickly she surmised that perhaps Dmitry had a reason to worry. When she returned to work, she made a search of CIA files and found Dmitry's name, which documented his status from student activist to communist and a potential spy for the Soviet Union. So, there it was, the two friends who were deeply interested in cetaceans and had avoided political discussions because of their very different political family histories had now discovered that they belonged to different organizations and that these organizations were at *war* with each other.

Dmitry recognized that both mentally and emotionally he was still attracted to Aurelia as a woman but her position at the CIA posed a real threat to him and his comrades and to the work he had started with dolphins. He recovered quickly from his initial shock that Aurelia's new job was at the CIA and had wished her good luck in her new position, smiling and shaking her hand, but he knew that she had noticed his reaction to her new job and was now likely suspicious of him. He told himself that in the future he would have to avoid any further discussions with Aurelia about dolphins; however, given what he wanted to do he quickly realized that avoiding talking with her about dolphins was going to be impossible.

Yes, Dmetri knew that he would eventually have to talk to Aurelia about dolphin communication because *if* it was possible that the two species could talk to each other about *conceptual* ideas, then this would be a major breakthrough in world history. Humans were sharing the planet with another species that biologically was very different, but the other species, the dolphins could also *think* and not just react to what they were perceiving. That truly would be historic and would rewrite history. The cold war between the Soviet Union and the West would be put to rest if both sides realized that dolphin abilities included understanding conceptional ideas. Certainly, Aurelia would understand this, and if she joined him, then together they could make history. But Dmitry realized he had to be careful. The CIA would have him and his comrades arrested, and someone like Sergei who carried a gun would be quick to use it.

(25) Voices of the Dolphins

Boris Volkov steered his cabin cruiser two miles into the Atlantic Ocean. The hot Florida sun scorched his bald head, and a salt spray watered his dry face. He thought of his wife and family in Moscow and wondered if the Russian weather was as harsh as when he had left years ago. On this particular day late in July, he enjoyed the perpetual summer of North Miami, Florida, where he now lived. He had now become acclimated to hot weather and was in the process of becoming an American citizen, but only on paper. Soviets can adjust to any situation was his thought.

Boris stopped the engine and allowed the boat to drift with the warm current. His eyes searched the ocean waves. Decaying garbage floated nearby. A whisky bottle bobbed and bumped against the boat. Even this far out, the pollution of the Americans could be seen was Boris's thought.

Suddenly a school of dolphins appeared. The sea mammals moved alongside the boat, and Boris smiled at the sight. Their grunts and clicks became louder and louder and turned into whistles as the air reverberated with their cries. Then, one by one, each dolphin leaped into the air sending forth a cacophony of high-pitched sounds. Using a portable tape recorder, Boris recorded these squeals – the voices of the dolphins.

This strange scene was repeated seven times. The dolphins circled the craft, leaping high above the water and the deck of the boat, and each dolphin squeaked into the recording microphone. Then as quickly as they had appeared, the dolphins disappeared into the ocean. Their sounds died away. Only the bumping of the whisky bottle against the boat could be heard above the waves as they now gently rocked his boat. Boris was alone, and he was excited. Another successfully completed assignment had been accomplished! The voices of these amazing sea mammals once again faithfully recorded as he had been doing ever since Sergei had introduced him to Dmitri. Today he recorded four tapes, including one where only a single dolphin had contributed its whistles and clicks, but that dolphin had returned six separate times to record its messages. The three other tapes were made by multiple dolphins, but each dolphin contributed only one or two squeals before departing.

Boris secured the tapes and drove the cabin cruiser back to North Miami and docked the boat. On shore, Boris became suspicious that a young man was watching him. The young man wore a blue shirt, gray slacks, and sported a small mustache. Always wary that the Americans were spying on him and his comrades, Boris quickly walked to his apartment and never looked back. He had only a few hours to organize the tapes he had recorded of the dolphin sounds and then pass the information to Comrade Dmitry. Once home, Boris locked the door behind him and hid the tapes behind a concealed wall board. If the man with the blue shirt and mustache broke into his apartment, he must not find and hear the recorded voices of the dolphins.

The next morning Boris, with the tapes in different pockets of his pants, went shopping at a grocery store where he found an empty cart. His first stop was to buy two apples, which went into a paper bag that the store provided along with the receipt that showed he had paid for them. As he wheeled the cart through the store, he saw Dmitry at the end of an aisle. Dmitry was also carrying a paper bag and holding a receipt. Boris took the two apples out of his bag and placed them into his cart, and as he walked slowly down the aisle, he took the tapes he had and placed them into the empty paper bag. When he got to Dmitry, he gave him the paper bag with the tapes and his receipt. Dmitry in turn placed his paper bag and receipt into the cart and continued walking, carrying the paper bag with the four hidden tapes and a receipt for two apples. The guard at the door just glanced at the receipt and never checked the contents of the paper bag. Dmitry went to his house to listen to the four tapes and attempted to understand what the whistles and clicks of the dolphins meant – he wanted to understand the voices of the dolphins.

Meanwhile, Boris placed the two apples into the bag that Dmitry had given him and went out another exit holding Dmitry's receipt. This was the routine they went through in order for Boris and Dmitry to exchange dolphin tapes. They knew they were likely being watched and did not want to be seen together at Dmitry's house or Boris's apartment. Thus, the dolphin tapes were passed back and forth in various grocery stores away from prying eyes. Dmitry would record a tape for the dolphins to listen to, and if they understood they would respond, and Boris would record their responses.

(26) Investigate Mic the Knife

On Tuesday July 11, 1972, Round 1 of the chess match between Bobby Fischer and Boris Spassky took place in Reykjavik, Iceland. This 'match of the century' was supposed to have started on Sunday, July 2, but it didn't. Bobby was holding out for more money, and a British chess promoter and financier, James Slater, came forward with an additional $125,000 to the prize fund. This doubled the amount that the Icelandic Chess Federation had put up and set the winner's purse at $156,250 and the loser's share at $93,750. That still didn't work for Fischer. Finally, after hours of persuasion, Bill Lombardy, Fischer's second and the fifth highest rated American chess player along with an attorney, Paul Marshall, finally got Bobby to agree to play this long-awaited match.

By this time Parker, Rosemary, and their four children were already in central Florida enjoying the delights of Disney World. Returning to their hotel at the end of the day, they and especially Peter, their twelve-year-old chess player, were disappointed to learn that Bobby Fischer playing the black pieces had uncharacteristically made two mistakes and lost the first game to Boris Spassky. "Fischer must be really nervous," said Peter, "you can't make mistakes like that in the middle game against Spassky - he's the World Champion!" After his loss, Bobby immediately complained that the television cameras were making noise, had distracted his thoughts, and demanded that the cameras be removed.

By the time all this was unfolding in the chess world, Parker had put Disney World and the chess match out of his mind to attend the scheduled meeting with Frank Jenkins and Aurelia Qundo at their CIA office in Orlando.

After the initial introductions, Frank gave Parker a folder and said Aurelia had done an analysis of Oscar's murder and had narrowed the likely killer down to either Edward Murray, the nephew of John Murray or a man by the name of Michael Klossmeier, also known on the street as Mic the Knife because he had stabbed someone and subsequently served time in prison. Another person of interest was Barry Snyder, who travelled frequently between the United States and Europe and likely carried information. However, the CIA thought Barry was only a courier for the Soviets and not a likely murderer.

For various reasons, the Agency did not want Chicago police involvement at this time, and they hoped Parker would agree to investigate both Edward and Mic independently of the police and build a solid case against one of them. If that happened, then that information would be turned over to the Chicago police. After that explanation, Frank thanked Parker and asked him to review the folder that had been prepared on the two men. Miss Qundo would answer most of the questions Parker had about the contents of the folder since she had done most of the work, but Frank would also chime in if appropriate.

The folder had Mic's mug shot at age 18 when he had been arrested for stabbing one of his senior classmates, a month after high school graduation. A second photo showed him five years later when he was released from prison. Prison had been tough on him and his face showed a much older man, smirking at the camera and missing one front tooth. Another photo was more recent, and an artificial tooth had been implanted. Moreover, it showed him next to a young woman, Marsha Dempsey, who wore very short shorts and a low-cut blouse. Marsha worked as a waitress at a local restaurant and lived with her mother, Delia, in a run-down house near the now defunct Chicago Stockyards. The mother also worked at the same restaurant, and they generally alternated shifts. They allowed Michael Klossmeier to live in their basement apartment after his release from prison, but neighbors hadn't seen Mic, as they called him, since early June. The last and most recent photo had a smiling Mic, seated at a wooden table, showing his new tooth. Next to him was a large knife stuck upright in the table. He seemed to be happy about both the tooth which he pointed at, and the knife, which held his gaze. Another recent police report indicated that he was receiving money from an unknown source in recent weeks, which might be an indication that he was being paid for the murder. Another report said it wasn't clear how he entered the Murray house the night of the murder unless Oscar had opened the front door and allowed the murderer to enter. This was possible, of course, if Oscar arranged the meeting and knew his murderer.

The folder on Edward showed his college graduation photo from the University of Chicago. Edward was on their fencing team. He could handle a sword quickly and with ease and therefore murdering someone by cutting their throat with a knife was believable. Additionally, he had a key to the house and could have entered at any time without raising any suspicion. As far as why he would commit a murder was unknown, but it was known that a recent project Edward worked on at the Argonne National Laboratory had been leaked to the Soviet Union. It wasn't clear who did this, but Edward was one of the suspects, and he was the only person on both CIA lists, the list of who might be spying and the list of possible murderers of Oscar.

The last item in the folder was the fee schedule that the Agency used to reimburse investigators like Parker who assisted them. Parker ignored this fee schedule, closed the folder, and startled both Frank and Aurelia when he immediately said, "I agree to investigate both Michael and Edward and help bring Oscar's murder to a conclusion."

"But you haven't heard any of the details about either of these men," said Frank looking at Aurelia who was also surprised by Parker's quick response.

"Frank," answered Parker, "at our last meeting, you said to me that the Agency was interested in trying to understand my sudden, unexpected insights that I had on cases. Well, at our prior meeting, I did have an insight regarding the CIA. The insight was: "*Miss Qundo and I would be involved not only in solving Oscar's murder but also in the revelation of a secret.*" Thus, I'm ready to start the investigation because I trust my insights based on my prior experience with such insights.

Both Jenkins and Qundo sat back in their chairs. Jenkins appeared amazed by the notion of an insight while Aurelia looked troubled. It was clear that Parker, revealing that he had a specific insight involving Miss Qundo, had caught the lady by surprise.

"Do you wish to continue, Miss Qundo?" asked Jenkins.

"Does your insight, Mr. Spooner, give any indication about the nature of the secret that we'll be revealing?" asked a cautious Aurelia looking directly at Parker. She remembered Parker had called her and told her about Boris Volkov and his boat visits out in the ocean.

"No, the two of us solving Oscar's murder was clear in my insight, but the nature of the revealed secret was not," answered Parker looking directly at Aurelia

"Who will come to know the secret? – you? me? Frank? the general public?" continued Aurelia.

"That's not clear to me, but I would think that at least you and I would know the secret since we're going to solve Oscar's murder. Of course, if the general public found out about a CIA secret, then that might be a problem for the Agency," said Parker. Based on Miss Qundo's questions, Parker was now reasonably certain that there was a CIA secret.

Frank and Aurelia looked at each other. Frank said, "Mr. Spooner wants this case, and I think we should proceed, Miss Qundo."

"I agree, Mr. Jenkins," responded Aurelia and with that Frank Jenkins left the room.

Aurelia started talking, "We think Oscar was likely murdered by either Michael Klossmeier or Edward Murray. We know some things about Michael because Oscar recently identified him as a possible spy. In particular, we believe the knife that cut Oscar's throat which left markings on his body would be consistent with the knife that Michael carries."

"What do you know about the knife that Michael carries?" asked Parker.

“When he was first arrested as a teenager for stabbing one of his buddies, the weapon was confiscated along with other evidence. That knife left certain striations in the victim’s skin. Now we need to find a knife which would be consistent with the wounds on Oscar. We think that Michael purchased a similar replacement knife after his release, and you saw a picture of Mic and that knife stuck upright in the table. We would like to obtain that particular knife, which we believe will match Oscar’s wounds.

“Do you know who manufactured that knife?” asked Parker.

“The name and manufacturer of that knife is given in the folder. It’s a German made weapon and unfortunately, I can’t pronounce any of the words,” said Aurelia, “but that brings me to another point, we think the killer slightly cut himself during the murder because we found a trace of AB- blood in the kitchen. That’s a rare type of blood, and Michael happens to be AB-. We have that information from Michael’s prior jail sentence. We found out Edward Murray’s blood type is also AB-, which is the reason that we haven’t eliminated him.”

“Okay, that’s interesting, Edward’s blood type matches as does Michael’s, but you also said Michael Klossmeier was on Oscar’s list. Do you know the reasons as to why Oscar had him there?”

“Not really, however, we know Soviet spies have been using runners to carry messages. The runner often doesn’t know he’s being used in such a manner. Oscar kept a list of such runners, and Michael was a recent addition to that list. Thus, we speculate that the Soviet spy had recently recruited Michael or Mic the Knife, and Oscar noted the new runner. It's even possible that Oscar contacted Mic and attempted to get evidence on the spy by inviting Mic to his apartment. Instead of giving Oscar evidence, Mic killed him."

"That would explain why Mic let the killer into his apartment," noted Parker, "but is there any evidence against Mic other than his blood type AB-?"

"Yes, Michael or Mic the Knife has come into quite a bit of money recently. It could be that money is his payoff for the murder, and Mic doesn't even realize that Oscar was a CIA agent."

"Has the CIA been able to trace where the payoff money is coming from?"

"No, it's one of those secret Swiss accounts. Right now it's not possible to say who's funding it, but it's likely the Russian government is supporting their spies in our country with money in Swiss accounts."

"Do you know who Mic hangs out with? Does he have friends or a crowd of guys that he associates with?" asked Parker.

"Yes, there's a list in the folder of his associates. It's not very long – Mic is pretty much a loner," responded Aurelia.

Parker found the list and looked at it. It had five names on it, including two that he recognized, David and Donald Glueck. Three others, Skip, Bruno, and Stever were Mic's neighbors. They helped each other, and this group went to Chicago White Sox baseball games together.

"This will be a good start for me," said Parker recognizing the Glueck' names, "and if I understand it correctly, the

CIA wants me to do surveillance of Michael Klossmeier and gather some evidence that he murdered Oscar. I would be working for the CIA in that capacity."

"Exactly, Mr. Spooner, we know you have resources who are able to watch and report on individuals and that you have successfully done that in the past. The Agency wants to hire you to do surveillance of Mic the Knife, which is Michael's street name and also Edward Murray, who had direct access to Oscar's apartment, and who may be the source of a leak at Argonne National Laboratories. Our only restriction is that your investigation should not directly involve police resources. In particular, Lieutenant Cambe's criticism of us was that we ignored the chain of police commands. He wants everything to funnel through him, but we're not going to do that. We operate independently and follow the laws of our country going through police channels when necessary. Given that Sergeant Boyle is your father-in-law and reports to Cambe that means that Sergeant Boyle is not going to know what we or what you are doing in this matter before the matter is made known to him through normal channels. Given that Sergeant Boyle is your father-in-law, will this be a problem for you or your resources, Mr. Spooner?"

"No, Miss Qundo," replied Parker, "that won't be a problem for my operatives or for me. We can keep any CIA secrets that we may learn to ourselves. I'm happy to accept your offer and consider myself hired by the CIA to investigate both Mic the Knife and Edward."

Aurelia reached out to shake Parker's hand. "Thank you, Mr. Spooner. We will reimburse your investigations according to the fee schedule in our folder." Parker shook Aurelia's hand and left the room. As Parker was leaving the CIA Orlando office, he waved goodbye to Frank Jenkins, who simultaneously was dictating a letter to a secretary and talking on the phone. Frank waved back with his free hand.

Meanwhile, Aurelia sat back in her chair, amazed at what just happened and by Parker himself. The CIA had allowed two hours for Parker's interview and within 30 minutes it was over and more had been accomplished than planned. Not only was Aurelia surprised that the Agency had likely found the right person to investigate Oscar's murder, but that Parker's demeanor was different from the other men she had encountered before joining the CIA. First, the fact that she was an attractive woman didn't seem to bother Parker in any way. She didn't pick up any innuendos, overt or suppressed, about her sex as the two sat together alone in a room. Second, he quickly grasped the essentials of the CIA's mission, and finally, his insight that the two of them collectively would solve Oscar's murder was believable. The one cause of worry was the secret mentioned within Parker's insight. Parker didn't know what the actual secret was, but his insight indicated that there was a secret. Miss Qundo wondered how the Agency would handle its secret if it became known. With those thoughts she joined Frank, who was no longer dictating a letter or talking on the phone.

"So, Miss Qundo, what do you think of Parker Spooner?" he asked.

"Favorable, but he's smart enough to find out what he calls a secret. That would be a problem for us would it not?"

"We would just classify all the papers. Parker's smart and wouldn't give away a CIA secret."

"It's strange but I think I've seen him somewhere before."

"He works exclusively in Chicago – how often have you been there?"

"The last time was four years ago at the Democratic National Convention – wait, that's it! He's the University of Chicago guy who helped me keep my class from going downtown the night the 1968 Convention turned into a street riot! Yet it's strange that he didn't mention that incident." She paused. "Perhaps he doesn't remember helping me control my students that night."

"No, Miss Qundo, Parker recognized you, but he wouldn't say anything and give away information. He's a private investigator and remains silent but observes, and I think we've found ourselves a good man."

Aurelia looked at Frank. He was smart and quick and ran the Miami CIA office with precision. Aurelia was in love with him, but he remained unmoved by the fact that she was a smart and a beautiful woman. He was all business, which was the CIA and its mission. Indeed, Frank thought he found a good man in Parker while Aurelia applied this good man description directly to Frank himself. '*He remains silent but observes. I think I've found myself a good man,*' was her own thought about Frank, and Aurelia was very happy working closely with him.

(27) Parker Begins His Investigation

Back home after their trip to Disney World, Parker called his two friends, Jim Rowdy and Ray Ulster, who had assisted him with surveillance in prior cases. Within a couple of days, they had verified that Mic the Knife had not been seen in Chicago since early June when he moved out of Delia Dempsey's apartment. They became aware that Mic and Delia's daughter, Marsha Dempsey, who also worked weekdays at the local restaurant, were friends. One Friday afternoon after Marsha left work, Jim Rowdy followed the Greyhound bus out of Chicago that she took to Madison where Marsha was greeted as she got off the bus by Michael Klossmeier. He had his green Studebaker and drove Marsha to his camper on the outskirts of the city where he was living. Jim noticed that the couple did not kiss but merely hugged each other.

Jim slept in his own car that night and was up early the next morning to follow the couple on Saturday. Around ten in the morning, Mic and Marsha arrived at a very nice vacant house located in an upscale part of Madison that had a large For Sale sign on its front lawn. A woman realtor arrived and ushered the couple inside where they were for about 30 minutes except for a brief excursion to view the back yard and then returning to the kitchen where the realtor had set up a small table and chairs. Standing on a side street with a pair of binoculars pretending to view bird nests scattered in the surrounding trees, Jim was able see that the realtor and Mic were signing paperwork while Marsha roamed through the rest of the house. The three of them then exited the house. The realtor, after locking the front door, hung an In Contract sign under the For Sale sign and then shook Mic's hand.

By this time, Ray Ulster had joined Jim. They decided that Ray would continue following Mic and Marsha while Jim would investigate the trailer park where Mic lived. Once there, Jim pretended that he was interested in Michael's trailer. He was informed by the camp's owner that particular trailer had been rented for the summer months, but Jim could have a similar trailer next to the one that he was interested in. Jim took the trailer park's phone number and information and after walking through the vacant trailer and said he would get back to them on Monday.

The next day was Sunday, July 23, and Jim and Ray met Parker at Parker's house in the afternoon to compare notes. Jim said Michael had just purchased a house in Madison. Jim also said that he could rent a trailer next door to where Michael was currently living in order to observe him in the future. Ray, in turn, indicated that Michael and Marsha had been running around various stores in Madison to buy things for the new house. Marsha seemed to be happy picking out curtains for multiple windows. Thus, both men confirmed that Michael had moved out of Chicago but had not severed his relationship with Marsha. The couple appeared to be high school friends, but not lovers. Neither Jim nor Ray could account for Mic's time the night of June 1 when Oscar was murdered, but it was immediately after that date that Mic started living in the trailer.

"Great job, gentlemen! Jim, hold off on renting that trailer since Mic just bought a house and will be moving soon. However, talk to his trailer neighbors and attempt to find out if they know anything about Michael," said Parker. "It seems that Michael came into money after the murder. If we could find out something about his source of money, we'd be on our way to solving who is behind the murder and the motive. Jim, the next time you're in Madison, try to find out who Mic is contacting or making friends with. Ray, please start talking to Mic's friends here in Chicago and find out what they know about him and Marsha. I'm going to visit Marsha's mother, Delia, when Marsha is at work in an attempt to gain some understanding of the arrangement these three people had when Mic was living in their basement.

"What are we do about Edward, the other guy, who may have murdered Oscar?" asked Jim.

"I've passed Argonne's security and will be going to visit them tomorrow to have lunch with Edward," replied Parker. "I'm also going to talk with the Glueck brothers soon since they're on the CIA's list of names." With that, the brief meeting of the three friends and investigators of Oscar's murder was over.

Later that evening after Jim and Ray had gone, Peter and his father talked about game 6 of the World Chess Championship that had just finished. Bobby Fischer had an exciting win and for the first time in the match took a one-game lead on Boris Spassky. This was an amazing comeback since after Bobby's game 1 opening round loss, he didn't show up for game 2 and was charged with a forfeit loss, going down 2-0 in the match. At that point, it appeared that the match was over and that Fischer, upset over the playing conditions, would not play anymore games. That set off a fury of activity behind the scenes to get Bobby back playing, which included a massive telegram campaign. Apparently, even Henry Kissinger, presidential advisor, got into the act and Bobby Fischer did show up and defeated Boris Spassky in game 3. It was the first time Bobby had ever defeated Boris. Game 4 was a draw, and then Fischer evened the match 2.5 to 2.5 with his second win in Game 5. That set up game 6, which turned out to be a beautiful classical win for Bobby that brought applause from the crowd. Even Boris Spassky, always the gentleman and a great World Champion, joined in the applause.

At age 12, Peter was so excited that his hero, Bobby Fischer, had taken the lead in the championship match that he was jumping around the house, running from chess set to chess set trying different variations, especially at the end of the game where Boris resigned because Bobby had a forced checkmate regardless of whatever move Boris might have made.

Parker, observing his son, decided to remind him what happened in the match after Fischer was down two games and about to quit playing further games. "Fortunately," the father said, "Bobby had the courage to believe in his ability to come from behind and thus he didn't quit."

Peter stopped jumping and thought about that and within a few seconds, he was seriously thinking about his own games at Gompers Park. "You know, Dad, I've never defeated Pavel Kotov. He's an adult and a good player, and he always picks up on my mistake and winds up winning the game."

"I remember your last loss to Mr. Kotov. You sacrificed a bishop for a pawn and an open rook file to his King, but that variation wasn't sound on your part. He could defend his King, and you were down a piece on your way to a loss."

“I know how to play that position now, and the bishop sacrifice is not part of the revised variation,” said an upbeat Peter.

“That’s good, Peter, stay with it, learn and change, and soon like Bobby, you will draw and then you’ll win a game against a player, like Pavel Kotov, that you never defeated before.”

Peter, encouraged by this thought, gave his father a big hug.

(28) Aurelia and Dmitry

Dmitry telephoned Aurelia and invited her to lunch. He said he wanted to talk about dolphin research similar to what they used to do as students. She accepted and they met at a restaurant near Dmitry's house in Miami. After they ordered, Dmitry said, "One of last times we talked about cetaceans you declined my offer to work together in order to communicate with them."

Aurelia smiled sheepishly, "Yes, I said we were a land species and dolphins were a water species and communications would be difficult to achieve."

"What would you say today given your current position?"

"I wouldn't make any comments at all."

"But, Aurelia, based on our prior work together, I think you could help me with scientific work that's important to humanity. I wish there would be some way that we could collaborate. What would be wrong with that?"

"Dmitry, I worry about you and pray for you, but I can't talk about my work, not only with you, but I can't talk about it with anyone. Furthermore, no romance between us is going to happen. I like you very much, but I don't love you."

With that a crestfallen Dmitry hung his head and asked, "Then you have a boyfriend, Aurelia?"

"No, I don't. I'm attracted to someone, and I love him, but he's far too busy to pay attention to me," replied Aurelia sadly.

"Then you're wasting your time with him," said Dmitry, raising his voice.

"Perhaps, but one cannot force love on a person," said Aurelia looking at Dmitry pointedly.

"I would never force you to do anything against your will, Aurelia," responded Dmitry softly.

"I believe you, Dmitry, but what about my will or the will of Cuban exiles concerning politics where you have strong opinions contrary to what we think. The Soviet Union forces many unwilling citizens to toe their line and just look at what Castro has done in my parents' homeland. They'll never forget having to flee Cuba, and they thank God every day for the United States of America. I know you once told me that you were disappointed in communism, but that's a mild criticism for all disruption that Castro done in Cuba."

"Cuba is a side show to the struggle that's going on in the world today, Aurelia. Eventually technology and leadership will eventually correct all injustice, and the world will come together," responded Dmitry.

"I hope so, but I doubt that, and it certainly won't be under communism if they continue to oppress people who disagree with them. Anyway, I would help you or anyone to better understand cetaceans and dolphins in particular," replied Aurelia, "but I won't help you with a non-scientific, oppressive ideology pushed by a foreign government."

"You're the one that recently joined a governmental agency," snapped Dmitry in an attempt to deflect her thoughts away from communism. "Did you not recently take a job at the Central Intelligence Agency?"

"Yes, but you're wrong about the Central Intelligence Agency being a governmental agency. The CIA is a *civilian* intelligence service. Its mission is to achieve national security through collecting and analyzing intelligence from around the world."

"You're naïve, Aurelia, if you believe that the American Government isn't running the Central Intelligence Agency," responded Dmitry. "The fact that they're technically civilian makes them even more dangerous because they commit illegal acts that the Government cannot do."

"If they break the law, then they should be arrested for committing illegal acts," responded Aurelia.

"But they're protected from being arrested and prosecuted because they're the CIA," said Dmitry.

Aurelia sighed deeply and said, "Look, Dmitry, I would just like to *learn* about dolphins and how they function in the oceans, and I also thought that was your motivation."

"It is, Aurelia, but at the same time, your agency has secret agents, and I don't think they are engaged in scientific research. For example, recently, I hear of an agent D. This CIA's agent D is currently the mystery agent who is doing something, somewhere, to someone, and I really doubt it has anything to do with research. However, I wouldn't doubt for a minute that Agent D may kill people."

"And foreign governments who have spies in the United States - are they doing research?" asked Aurelia.

"I'm doing research, Aurelia," said Dmitry.

"And so am I, on dolphins – is it possible for you to share such information on dolphins with me, Dmitry?" asked Aurelia.

"I can't tell you specific details because the research is still going on and much of it has not been substantiated. Let me ask you, Aurelia, has your Agency successfully started communicating with dolphins as the two of us once tried to do with a tape recorder?"

"That would be classified information if we did," replied Aurelia, "but I believe you may have successfully communicated with them because you never stopped trying. If so, I was wrong back then when I thought it was a waste of time, and it couldn't be done."

"But the specific details of what is now known about dolphins is the issue, and that's what's on my mind," said Dmitry.

"Dmitry, you just said you can't tell me specific details of your research because it's ongoing, and that's also my response to you."

Dmitry hung his head.

Aurelia looked at Dmitry sadly. He was a grown man but in many ways his mind was innocent like that of a child when it came to politics and the evil done by some when they obtained political power. In particular, Dmitry was oblivious to the evils that communism had inflicted on the world. She merely said to him, "I like you very much, Dmitry, and hope that what we collectively discover about dolphins can work for the benefit of all life on this planet."

Dmitry looked at her for a long time and finally responded, "Let me think further about this, Aurelia."

It would take some time, but eventually Dmitry and Aurelia would be back together having lunch and discussing their dolphin research, but for now that was not happening.

(29) Dmitry Transcribes

In his house, Dmitry listened to the tape of the dolphins that Boris had recorded earlier in the week. Their squeaks could be heard above the sound of the sea. Dmitry slowed down the tape so that he could distinctly hear each note of their chorus. Carefully he transcribed their message onto paper. The language experts in Moscow would then translate the Dolphin sounds into Russian and then attempt to understand what the mammals were saying. It was demanding work, and Dmitry sighed, listening and rewinding the tape again and again, to record the proper pitch of each dolphin's whistle. Dmitry’s head nearly touched the speaker as he strained to hear properly. He would work the entire night, if necessary, to get the entire written message correctly and delivered overseas by plane in the morning. If the frequency of the dolphin whistle wasn’t correct, then the message would be confusing, perhaps impossible to understand.

Dmitry wondered how many years Russians had studied the dolphins before the two species started to communicate, which was a very recent and confusing development. The Soviets found the dolphins intelligent but totally innocent like a happy child without any political notions or ambitions. Each dolphin apparently was content within his own being and helped other dolphins when asked. Thus, the goal of the Russians was to have dolphins along the Florida coast spying on American military movements, and the dolphins would do this because the Soviets had merely requested this from them. It all depended on recording and understanding the particular frequency of the various whistles and clicks that came from the dolphins. If done correctly, then from the space center at Cape Kennedy down to the naval base at Key West, dolphins would keep watch on the Americans. In this way, it was thought that valuable facts would be revealed to Soviet intelligence. Indeed, the Soviet hope was that dolphins would gather better information about the Americans than the entire fleet of Russian trawlers and fishing vessels combined.

However, Boris, after watching and interacting with the dolphins from his boat, told Dmitry that he feared that these mammals were smarter than men. He knew that they were friendly and when they came up to his boat, he could distinguish one from another by looking into their eyes and that fact frightened him. He knew that some scientists felt dolphins were a major evolutionary line because of their larger cerebral cortex than humans. Furthermore, the cetacean brain was divided into more layers that allowed them to integrate rational and emotional impulses better than humans. In this view man was an overspecialized trend doomed to self-extinction because of internal egocentric forces. One theory held that each dolphin could solve rational problems and philosophically think completely satisfied within its own brain as it interacted with the world as it was. This species did not need human technology because their technology was already built within the species. Thus, when a man wanted a dolphin to jump through a hoop or catch a thrown fish, then the completely satisfied, independent ocean species would joyfully amuse the always searching game-playing warlike land species.

Comrade Boris shuddered at these heretical thoughts but conveyed them to Dmitry, who also worried about the state of the world. To divert his mind on this day, Dmitry snapped on the radio in his house. "Tonight, the Soviet Union reported the launch of a space satellite ……," said the announcer. Dmitry smiled. Yes, it was good to be reminded! He remembered how he felt and why he joined the Communist Party. How silly of him to worry about dolphins! It did not matter one way or the other if dolphins did or did not realize that they were aiding a world revolution and a noble cause when they reported information. Dmitry initial belief was that Soviet science and technology would improve the lot of all people and someday dominate the planet. Industrial and social progress would be theirs. Even now Soviet scientists were likely working on projects that would change the world. They would orbit space laboratories and use robots to explore the solar system. They would plant high protein grains. They would melt the Arctic ice and turn Siberia into a sub-tropical zone.

The radio announcer continued, "The Department of Agriculture said today that 150,000 acres of pasture land in central Florida were irreparably damaged. The recent rapid growth of the area had pushed the finite resources limits to the point of collapse …" droned the emotionalist announcer. Dmitry turned off the radio. He knew that the surge of past feelings that he had just experienced were all *incorrect*. Both the capitalists and his comrades were *incorrect*! Things were not going well – they were not going the *right* way - not in the Soviet Union or in America or in the world - and the attempt to involve the dolphin species by either side was wrong!

Dmitry could not have known that the dolphins Boris had interacted with earlier and that their whistles and clicks that he was now translating into human language were subsequently joined by a much larger dolphin as they moved north in the ocean heading toward Cape Kennedy. Dolphins have limited eyesight underwater but use sonar-like devices that are part of their bodies to see objects. Like ultrasound used in medicine by humans, dolphin sonar allows them to see the internal workings of other animals.

They can read emotions and states of health in other creatures and project auditory images that replicate the sonar messages. This large dolphin had conveyed holographic images to the other dolphins that caused them to stop their journey.

(30) Gorky Genkin

Gorky Genkin was one of Sergei's new operatives and had been assigned to the South of Florida to help Dmitry translate the dolphin language into human language. To get up to speed as to what was happening, Gorky joined Boris on one of his trips to the Atlantic Ocean to record the dolphin whistles and clicks. "Once that's done," said Boris, "I give the tapes to Dmitry who acts on the information and prepares responses. You'll be helping him with those responses."

Gorky then watched as Boris back on land marked and sorted the new tapes to give to Dmitry who, in turn, would carefully listen to the tapes and transcribe the dolphin sounds into English letters and words. Additionally, if Dmitry had made any tapes that would instruct the dolphins as to what they were to do, he would give these new tapes to Boris to play the next time he went out into the ocean to locate the dolphins.

"Yes," said Gorky, "now that I see what you're doing, I'll be contacting Dmitry. Apparently preparing a response that the dolphins can understand and act upon is a difficult task."

"Yes, but we're slowly learning and hopefully you'll speed up the process."

"Nevertheless, none of this makes much sense to me. I don't understand why Sergei or his bosses moved me down here. Anyway, I've got my gun, and I'm not afraid to use it if something unexpected happens," said Gorky with a forceful voice as he said goodbye to Boris.

The next day, Gorky went to Dmitry's house. One of the first things he conveyed to Dmitry was his last comment to Boris. Dmitry shook his head, "There'll be no need to use a gun here. We've started a process of learning how to communicate with another species."

Gorky smirked, "If the CIA interferes with your plans, you'll need a gun."

Dmitry frowned and changed the subject, "Let me show you what I'm currently working on and where I need help. Here are two tapes that will be given to Boris to play when he sees dolphins. The first tape is marked Alpha; that's the name of a specific dolphin we've identified. The second tape is marked Beta for another identified dolphin. Boris will play the first tape when he spots Alpha and the second when he sees Beta."

"He can actually tell them apart?" said a skeptical Gorky.

"Yes, their facial features are different."

"What happens after he plays the tape?"

"If the messages are coded correctly and understood, then each dolphin will do what we requested."

"And what's that?"

"We are asking each of them to go up to Cape Kennedy, get close and observe from the water, and then report on what the Americans are preparing for their next launch."

"What, are you crazy?" said a smirking Gorky.

"No, we believe the dolphins can do this if the message I'm sending is coded properly."

"I thought we were merely sending Russian trawlers with their sound equipment to cruise past the place in order to keep a watch on what's going on along the coast," said an amazed Gorky.

"The dolphins can get in closer and what they pick up and then repeat for us hasn't been jammed or modified. This is just another test to see what's possible with dolphins."

Gorky just shook his head, "What do want me to do with all of this stuff?"

Dmitry loaded a tape on his recorder and pressed the play button, "This is the tape for Alpha. The same message will be played three times." Dolphin whistles and clicks were heard followed by a couple of squeals. There was a long pause and then the whistles, clicks, and squeals repeated followed by the pause and then there was the third playing of the same message.

"And what, Comrade Dmitry, am I supposed to do in all of this?" repeated Gorky.

"First of all, you'll have to learn what we discovered about the Dolphin language. I've prepared written instructions and several tapes explaining their basic language. You'll spend a few days learning this before we ask you to decode new dolphin messages coming in. Once you've done that, then you'll be ready to prepare tapes like the one you just heard. That's the most difficult, recording a message to the dolphins and having the dolphins actually do what you've instructed them to do."

"I don't know about all this, Comrade. I thought I'd be seeing some action down here."

"This is important action, Comrade," replied Dmitry. "The dolphins can be trained as spies and do the work better than our trawlers, and if we can actually learn to communicate with them about conceptional ideas, then the world will be changed."

Gorky smirked but said, "Okay, show me the instruction books and tapes, and let me get started,"

Dmitry did that, but it was clear that Gorky Genkin was not happy about his new assignment, and thus, it was no surprise that a day later, Sergei stopped by Dmitry's house to talk.

"Comrade Genkin is finding this new assignment too speculative and without any action," said Sergei. "I told him that our Comrades in Moscow and those in charge here in the States, consider the project to train dolphins to spy for us as a top priority. However, I recognize that Gorky needs some space to roam, so I suggested he discreetly walk around the docks and occasionally go out with Boris to visit the dolphins. If he actually saw Alpha of Beta up close, and they him, then I think his view would change. Anyway, Boris tells me he expects to see both Alpha and Beta tomorrow, so Gorky will be joining him on the boat. We'll see if that works to ease his unrest."

"Yes, we'll see if that helps Gorky," answered Dmitry, who was becoming more and more annoyed with Sergei and how his counterparts were handling attempts to communicate with dolphins. They clearly wanted to train the dolphins to become Soviet spies, while Dmitry's goal was attempting to reach the dolphins as conceptional thinkers. That didn't seem to be part of the Soviet plan, or if it was, it was getting lost.

The next morning Boris and Gorky were out on the ocean. When Boris got to a certain spot, he looked at his watch, and then shading his eyes he glanced at the position of the sun. He then cut off the engine and the boat started drifting. "They'll be here soon," he said to Gorky. "I expect that both Alpha and Beta will be among the dolphins. If so, I have a special tape here to get their attention. I mention your first name on the tape, and I'm hoping to introduce you to them." Boris put the tape into the tape deck, and as soon as the dolphins approached, he started playing the tape. The dolphins started leaping out of the water, squealing their greetings above the boat. Boris grabbed the arm of Gorky and pulled him up to show him to the leaping dolphins. "There's Alpha and there's Beta" shouted Boris as those two dolphins appeared. He turned up the volume of the tape. "If they catch the message, they'll come to the side of the boat to see you, Gorky."

Sure enough, Boris was correct and a minute later, there were two dolphins along the side of the boat. Boris grabbed Gorky with one hand and pointed at him with his other hand as the two dolphins briefly raised themselves above the water to see over the side of the boat and view Gorky. Boris was screaming with delight, "We did it! Gorky you've met Alpha and Beta!"

Gorky looked stunned. Since arriving in Miami a few days ago, his world view was changing. "What's going on here with these dolphins?"

"They now know who you are, Gorky," said Boris. "They know you're involved in the back and forth between dolphins and humans that's now taking place."

Gorky wasn't certain if that was a good thing or not and asked, "Are they Russian dolphins or American dolphins?

"They're greeting us and communicating with us, and we're Russian," said Boris.

"But they're in American water," responded Gorky.

Boris frowned. He didn't know how to respond and said nothing.

At this moment, Gorky was looking at the ocean and noticed an enormous sized dolphin next to the boat. He couldn't help letting a Russian expletive come out of his mouth. Gorky saw the dolphin's eyes, and the creature was looking directly up at him.

Boris looked down and saw the oversized mammal. "Wow, I've never seen one this size. What's it doing here?"

With that, the dolphin submerged out of sight, leaving a wave that rocked the boat.

"That creature was looking at me!" shouted Gorky. "It's like he knew me and wanted to inspect me."

Boris laughed. "That was a surprise, but I really don't think he was looking at you."

"You didn't see his eyes!" shouted Gorky.

"I think they use sonar to see," replied Boris.

"Okay, then that creature saw me with sonar!"

Back on land, Gorky started walking along the Florida piers, and he would talk to people and find out what they knew, if anything, about dolphins. Most of the time he was just ignored, but occasionally he found someone willing to discuss the docks and dolphins. He learned that it was rare for a dolphin to come close to the shoreline. A person would have to rent a boat and go out in the ocean to see dolphins. Gorgy bumped into a man who kept touching his mustache and who directed him to a pier that went quite far out into the ocean. Mustache said that was the best bet for seeing a dolphin in the wild. Gorky made the long walk, came to the end of the pier, and looked at the ocean that stretched out in front of him all the way to the horizon. He didn't see any dolphins, but he would return later.

Meanwhile, all the ocean work being done by Boris was being followed closely by the CIA. Williams, who was watching the docks, reported that a new person had joined Boris on some of his boat trips and also did extensive walking on the docks looking for dolphins. Based on a description of Gorky, Special Agent Jenkins had Miss Qundo do a search of their files and soon information about Gorky Genkin was available. He was a notorious killer in Russia and then Europe, quick to use his gun, and somehow the Soviets had gotten him into America. Jenkins swore to himself wondering why America was careless when it came to Soviet immigration. "They're adding killers to their spies and have now added a person who enjoys using his gun to kill people. The Russians somehow had hidden this killer's background in order to place him here. We need to act on this quickly. Since Gorky is walking on the docks that stretch out into the ocean, that's Agent D territory and I'll get him involved in dealing with Gorky," said Jenkins to Miss Qundo.

Aurelia looked at her boss to see if Jenkins wanted her to get involved with this new agent. Thus far, the identity of Agent D was known only to Jenkins. "I'll be taking care of this myself, Miss Qundo, thank you." Aurelia nodded and left Jenkins' office. Once again, Agent D would remain unknown to everyone at the CIA except Special Agent Jenkins.

Several mornings later, Boris waited in his boat for Gorky, but he never showed up, and thus, Boris went out by himself into the ocean steering his boat, *1922*. Boris was worried. He knew something had happened because Gorky was always ready to leave early. Several hours later when *1922* returned to the pier Boris was approached by a solemn Dmitry, "Gorky was found drowned off one of the piers early this morning. He had drawn his pistol, which was found on top of the pier. It hadn't been discharged, but Gorky was floating dead in the water. The police said he drowned. The police think he slipped, hit his head, and fell into the water after dropping his gun on the deck. In any case, we'll have to shut down our operation for a couple of days. The police will be questioning you, Boris, as to why he was using your boat. Remember our cover story. He was just some stranger who was interested in possibly settling in this area and wanted to become familiar with the area by viewing the coastline from Fort Lauderdale all the way down to the Keys, and for a small fee, your boat took him out on the ocean."

Boris nodded, but he certainly didn't believe that Gorky had slipped and then drowned.

(31) Parker Talks to Edward

Parker arrived at the Argonne National Laboratory in Lemont, Illinois, slightly before noon, parked his car, checked in, received a badge, and met Edward in their cafeteria. They took a table at the edge of the cafeteria next to a window that viewed the parking area.

"Why do you want to talk to me, Mr. Spooner?"

"Let's go back to the night of Oscar's murder. You were not at your uncle's house that evening because you were here in Lemont at your apartment."

"That's correct."

"The front door of your uncle's house is locked and neither John nor Ruthy opened the door that night nor did they hear anyone ring the outside bell. This means Oscar expected someone at a certain time and came down the steps to let a person in and they walked up the stairs unheard by your aunt and uncle."

"That's fairly easy to do especially if my aunt and uncle are in their bedroom. They're normally in bed and asleep by eleven o'clock."

"Now Oscar had withdrawn money from the bank and was about to pay someone $10,000 for some information," said Parker.

Edward looked genuinely surprised at this development, "I didn't know that."

"Okay, now you know. What information do you think he was buying?"

"How in the world would I know?" said Edward, who appeared unnerved.

"Suppose he was buying United States classified information."

Edward sat straight up in his chair. "I wouldn't know anything about that."

"Of course not, Edward, I'm not thinking that you would, even though I understand some of your work might be classified. I'm merely pointing out that Oscar's murder raises many possibilities."

"Yes, I see what you mean. I work in an area where I do work that's classified and now the guy living in my uncle's place where I also live part-time is murdered. This guy is also engaged in some sort of buying information as a spy. Now because of the murder, everyone is looking at me and my work at Argonne. Did my work have something to do with Oscar's death?"

Parker said to Edward, "That's it, Edward. "I'm investigating Oscar's murder and want to apprehend whoever did it. If there's anything you wish to convey that could help me with my task, I would appreciate it."

"Good luck, but don't look at me, Parker, I didn't murder him nor do I have any idea who did or what the motive was," said Edward.

"Oscar was about to reveal a Soviet spy. Perhaps he was buying information that would identify the spy. Instead of providing information to Oscar, the person killed him and took the money," said Parker.

"I don't know anything about Oscar and what he was doing. I'm not a spy. If the classified project I worked on was leaked, I don't know who leaked it. It wasn't me."

"I'm going to be leaving, Edward, but here's what I'm going to do before I go. I'll tell you what you were working on in six words before I leave, and then I'll immediately leave after I disclose to you what your classified project did. That is, I'll mention your secret project quietly in six words without going into any details. If I'm correct, you don't have to say anything. I'll just get up and leave. If I'm wrong, then please tell me if I'm wrong before I leave. In either case, I don't think I'll bother you again. Would you be willing to do that?"

"You'll describe my classified project in six words?" said an incredulous Edward, "And you want an agreement on my part that if you've described it accurately in those six words, I'd remain silent. However, if you're wrong with those six words, then I would tell you that you're wrong. In either case, whether your six words describe the project or not, you'll be leaving and won't be back to bother me."

"That's correct, Edward. Would you be agreeable to that arrangement?"

"Of course, let me hear your six words!"

Parker leaned in, and quietly looking at Edward's eyes said, "An electronic translator of cetacean sounds."

Edward sat back in his seat; his mouth opened in amazement, but he spoke no words. That was the name of his classified project!

“Thank you,” said a smiling Parker as he got up and left a silent Edward at a lunch table in the Argonne National Laboratory cafeteria.

Edward hung his head. He knew he had given away his project that night at O’Rourke’s. He knew he had to admit his mistake and amend his life.

(32) Parker Talks to Delia and Marsha

It was mid-morning the next day when Parker rang Delia's doorbell. He knew she was at home and that Marsha, her daughter, was working at the restaurant. When Delia opened the door, Parker, who was wearing a suit and tie, introduced himself as an independent private investigator not affiliated with the police and showed his credentials. There remained a screen door between them. "I would like to talk to you about Michael Klossmeier, Mrs. Dempsey. It should not take too long. May I come in and sit?" asked Parker.

Delia, who had been expecting a visit from someone regarding Michael, unlocked the screen door and showed Parker a seat on a small couch that faced a television set on a stand. She locked the screen door but did not close the main door allowing the outside to be viewed. Delia then turned off the TV and pulled up a chair to face Parker across a small table in front of the couch. The room was small but clean and uncluttered. Off to the side, Parker could see the kitchen and a closed door, probably to a bedroom and bathroom.

Delia looked at Parker. She had decided to talk to him and didn't slam the door in his face, which had been her initial thought. Delia was concerned about her daughter and thought perhaps she could get information from this investigator that would help her in dealing with Marsha and Michael. "What do you want to know about Michael Klossmeier?" she asked.

"I know that Michael is now living in Madison, Wisconsin, and your daughter, Marsha, visits him on some weekends. I wonder if you would tell me your opinion of Michael?"

Delia looked surprised. She had not expected this type of question. “What do you mean by my opinion of him?”

“Can you tell me as a mother of your daughter your opinion of Michael? Is he a good man? Is he kind to your daughter? Does he treat her properly?”

Delia was surprised these questions, “My daughter seems to be happy with him; however, we know he was in jail for stabbing a man. However, Marsha believes all of that is behind him now – he was young and immature when that happened.” Delia didn’t sound convinced, and her look showed it. She continued, “I’m hoping for the best now. What do you know about Michael?”

“Not very much, however, I’m wondering if you know when he moved from Chicago to Madison. In particular, was he still here in Chicago late Wednesday night May 31 going into Thursday, June 1?”

“That’s several weeks ago, I wouldn’t remember – well, wait a minute. That is the night he left to drive to Madison, Wisconsin. That’s right – it was the end of the month, May 31, and he took off in his Studebaker that he had just fixed. Marsha went up to Madison on a couple of weekends but that didn’t happen this past weekend.” Delia paused and then added. “I’m not crazy about Michael and hope his relationship with my daughter is ending.”

Parker nodded to acknowledge her last comment and then continued, “What time do you think Michael left your place the night of May 31?”

“About nine because it was already dark,” said Delia.

Parker had just learned something important from Delia; namely, Michael had left her place the night of the murder!

Certainly, Mic had plenty of time to drive to the Murray house and kill Oscar before driving to Madison. Now if he did stop at the Murray house and killed Oscar on his way up to Madison, then what was his motive? Had he known Oscar before and was this some sort of a revenge killing or had he been hired to kill Oscar? Why did Oscar open the front door and allow the killer into his apartment? Parker decided to probe further.

"Thank you, Mrs. Dempsey, for your time and for answering my questions. Did Michael ever mention the name, Oscar Busby, to you?"

"No, I don't know that name, but Michael didn't talk about people."

"He also seems to have come into money recently. Did you notice that?" Parker was thinking not only of the $10,000 cash Oscar had on him the night of the murder but also the money he may have received if he was under contract to murder Oscar.

"Yes, Michael's bought a house in Madison, which surprised me. I didn't think he had much money when he got out of jail and rented our basement."

"Something apparently has happened to give him money to buy a house," offered Parker, "Your daughter hasn't said anything to you about him or the house?"

"Not really, I don't believe she was thinking about marrying him, and I hope he didn't play her for a fool although he probably tried. I think she was just interested in traveling and visiting Madison to get away. I think she's bored with being a waitress. She's a bright woman and goes to night school." She paused and said with a worried look, "Why are you investigating Michael"?

" I wouldn't want to needlessly alarm you and your daughter, and it would be inappropriate for me to say anything about my inquiry other than it's unlikely that your daughter is in any direct immediate physical danger from Michael. I cannot speak to her emotional state or what her heart may long for in her relationship with Michael, nor can I speculate about Michael's new found money."

Mrs. Dempsey liked Parker and decided to level with him, "I wish Marsha would go back to her high school sweetheart, Jim Leaver. He's a hard working guy and has a good job with an insurance company. Michael Klossmeier troubles me but thank you for telling me that Marsha isn't in any immediate physical danger from him. However, I worry about her especially if he's doing something against the law. I don't want her to make a mistake, but I can't talk to her about Michael without causing an argument."

Parker understood how Delia felt about her daughter and asked, "I need to talk to Marsha about Michael just as I have with you. When will she be here at home?"

"She will be back at 1:30 today, and I'll be off to take her place at the restaurant for the rest of the day."

"That's in less than an hour, Mrs. Dempsey. I can wait for her if that would be possible from your point of view."

"That would be wonderful, Mr. Spooner. You can watch TV if you want. It won't take me long to get ready and arrive at the restaurant. I'll send Marsha back immediately." Parker nodded with his assent. Delia turned on the TV for Parker, went to change clothes, and then went off to the restaurant.

as she took a seat on the other side of the table.

Shortly after 1:30 pm, a lively Marsha bounded into the house, "My mother told me you were here. Let me get out of my waitress clothes and into something more comfortable." She spoke clearly and with confidence. She went into the bedroom, and a few minutes later she came out dressed casually wearing shorts and a blouse. "Mother tells me your name is Parker Spooner, and you're a private investigator looking for information about Michael Klossmeier." Based on the way she talked and handled herself, taking a seat on the other side of the table, it was clear to Parker that Marsha was an intelligent young woman.

"That's correct," replied Parker, "I've learned that he moved out of your mother's apartment at the end of May and he's bought a house in Madison, Wisconsin. You've been up there a couple of times on weekends."

"Yes, he's been living in a trailer park, waiting for the house to close and its occupants to move out. I wasn't up there this past weekend, but the closing is going to happen this Friday, and I'm supposed to visit him this weekend"

"Buying a house must be quite an expense for Michael."

Marsha frowned, "Yes, and that bothers me. Mic got angry at me for asking him about how he's paying for the house."

"Did he give you any kind of answer?"

"None at all. He just told me to shut up and not worry about it. He's a man and will take care of it. That's his attitude." Marsha hung her head and was clearly annoyed by this. Parker remained silent, and Marsha then added, "I don't understand how Mic got the money to buy a house. At first,

I thought his family had money, but then I found out that's not the case. He grew up poor. So, I don't know how he can afford a house. Is that why you're investigating him?"

"Yes, that's part of my investigation, which also involves a serious crime."

Marsha sat up straight, wide eyed and now looked frightened, "Not murder, dear Lord, I hope the crime is not murder? Tell me, what's the crime?"

"Sadly, Miss, the crime is murder - a man's throat was cut with a knife," said Parker.

Marsha hung her head, hands to her face, "I knew something was very wrong, but murder, oh no, Michael, no! What have you done!" She said this with anger and began crying. Parker sat there and allowed her to cry.

Almost immediately, Marsha snapped out of it and said, "That's it, I'm definitely going to break it off with him. I knew something was wrong, but this settles it. Two days ago, I talked to my old boyfriend, Jim Leaver, and the contrast between Jim and Mic is stark. I used to think of Jim as boring, but he's a kind and generous person. I realized that I made a mistake with Jim, and this clinches it. I hope it's not too late to get Jim back. I don't think it is."

"Michael Klossmeier has not been charged or convicted of any crime, Miss Dempsey," said Parker, surprised by this turnaround.

"I know, and I truly hope Mic is innocent of murder, but I've been thinking about leaving him for some time and when I saw Jim Leaver it struck me that I had been too hasty and actually stupid in thinking of Jim as dull and boring. He's a great guy, and I sensed it when I saw him again and truly, I've been thinking about Jim since. I'm going to call him and see if we can get back together."

"And, if he says no?" asked Parker.

"I'll be sad and kicking myself for not having recognized his strengths earlier, but I know that after this experience, I'll be looking for the 'Jim's' in this world and not taken in by the 'Mic's'. I'm definitely dumping Mic the next time I see him."

Parker was delighted at this development and decided to press forward. If she was really serious and done with Mic, then perhaps she would help with his investigation. Parker had purchased a new knife identical to the one Mic currently had and showed it to Marsha. He then showed her a used knife, which looked identical to the new one except that the sheath that held the used knife was slightly worn.

"I would like you to help me obtain evidence against Michael. Would you be willing to do that?"

"Marsha was now excited, "Yes, what do you want me to do?"

"What I'm going to ask you to do Miss Dempsey could be very dangerous so if you said no I would completely understand, but I would like you to take these two knifes with you the next time you visit Michael but keep them hidden. If possible, when you're alone, replace the knife Mic currently has with one of the two knives that I'm giving you. You'll use which ever knife best matches his current knife."

"I can do that," said a confident Marsha.

Parker continued, "Now the sheath of Mic's current knife shouldn't be replaced at all. You'll be leaving that sheath with Mic and only replacing his knife. When looking at the sheath and the protruding new knife handle, it's only the handle of the new knife that might give the exchange away. Thus, when you make the switch, you need to look carefully at Mic's current knife and replace it with one of the two knives I'm giving you. I expect one of those knives will be a very close match to Mic's actual knife because he just purchased that knife when he got out of prison, and I just bought these two. In any case, take the knife that best matches Mic's knife and place it in Mic's current sheath. Clearly, if neither of the two knives is close to the one you're taking, then do not make any switch at all. Without a match, you would leave Mic's knife in place! It's Mic's current knife that you are taking from him and bringing it back to me so that a police lab can test it and see if it matches the murder weapon."

"Yes, I understand. I'll be returning with two knives and Mic's knife that I took by the switch will be the one that will be tested," said Marsha. "I wonder if his knife will show any evidence that it's the murder weapon?"

"A microscopic, dried blood dot might still be on the knife if it's the murder weapon and if it hasn't been perfectly cleaned. Also, these knives are made by machines, but the grooves on any given knife will minutely vary and if his knife is the murder weapon, we'll likely be able to identify it," answered Parker.

"Weeks ago, I thought Mic was an exciting person and had put stabbing people or harming someone behind him, but that's not true. Now instead of being by his side, I might be sending him to prison for life," said Marsha.

"If you can make the switch this weekend, I'll return next Monday and drive you to the police station so that you can give them the knife and make a statement." Marsha enthusiastically nodded yes. She was very excited about what she was going to do. Parker thought this young woman was bright and would handle the retrieval of Mic's knife with care.

(33) Edward Confesses

Edward Murray telephoned Parker and asked for an appointment at Parker's office, saying it was important and had to do with 'an electronic translator of cetacean sounds'. Parker told him to come to his office after Edward was done working at Argonne for the day. "It will be late, Parker, because I work to 5:00 pm, and it's a distance to get to Hyde Park from Lemont during rush hour, but I'll be there."

"I'll be waiting for you," said Parker.

And thus, Edward showed up and told Parker the story of how he had been tricked by this guy, Dmitry Doby. Somehow, over a period of Fridays at O'Rourke's tavern Edward had revealed secrets about the workings of the electronic translator that Argonne was developing. He had been really stupid and on that last Friday when he returned the corrected diagram to Dmitry it was late at night and he was drunk. But that corrected diagram, if used, would produce the electronic translator of cetacean sounds. Dmitry hadn't asked him about it or forced him in anyway. Dmitry said that this information was for engineers at Brookfield Zoo's Dolphinarium, and Edward thought it would open up opportunities for him if they recognized what he had done in developing the translator. Now Edward expected to be fired, if not prosecuted for giving away classified information.

"So, what are you going to do?" asked Parker.

"I'm going to resign, confess, and get a job teaching, assuming that Argonne won't try to prosecute me. Hopefully, this electronic translator that I helped design will not make a decisive difference in the balance of power since the Soviets were also working on it and would have eventually figured it out. Both sides will have it and be using it."

"Exactly what does this "translator of cetacean sounds" do?" asked Parker.

"It takes the various vocal sounds that dolphins make and turns it into an English word or if the word has syllables which most words do then an English syllable. We are slowly learning the dolphin language, and they or some dolphins are learning English. I think the Russians are teaching them Russian and that may be confusing them and slowing down the communication process among dolphins."

"In any case, dolphin communication sounds like it would be a long and difficult process," mused Parker.

"Yes, I believe it is," agreed Edward.

Parker wondered if even perceptual words might be difficult for humans to convey to dolphins because dolphins were living in the oceans away from sunlight and did not experience sight the way humans living on land did. Yet dolphins did perform well in daylight at dolphinariums. Parker realized he didn't understand how this species actually functioned.

"All the best to you, Edward," said Parker shaking Edward's hand.

(34) Parker Talks to the Glueck Brothers

Parker walked into the Glueck Brothers Jeweler store. Donald Glueck was at the counter, "May I help you, sir.?" There was no one else in the store except Parker caught a glimpse of David, the older brother rummaging around in a back room.

This was a perfect time to talk to both of them together and not have to worry about other ears listening thought Parker who quickly responded, "I'm a private investigator and would like to talk to you and your brother together."

"Come on out, David. We have a private gumshoe here who wants to talk to us," shouted Donald for his brother.

David pushed aside the curtain that separated the two rooms, "What's going on?"

"I'm Parker Spooner, a private investigator, and have a couple of questions about Oscar Busby, who was recently murdered."

"Yeh, we knew Oscar – that happened weeks ago. What do you want to know?" asked David.

"Oscar took bets on sporting events. Kept records on everything in a black book. The night of the murder, Oscar had 10 grand with him. He was buying info on something for someone. Now here's a fact that's not known or reported in the press and that's Oscar was also working for the United States Central Intelligence Agency. Because of that fact, the thought is that Oscar may have been murdered because of his CIA connection, and the Russians may have been involved in his murder. Now this is a long shot on my part, but I'm wondering if you guys know anything at all about Oscar or who might have been selling him information the night he was murdered."

The two brothers looked genuinely shocked at what Parker had just said to them. They then exchanged glances, looking at each other puzzled, and finally David said to Parker "Go outside the store for a moment. I want to talk to my brother alone." Parker complied and stood on the outside sidewalk. Looking through the window, he could see the two brothers talking and waving their hands. He recognized that what he had just done was a gamble, but his instinct was that local thieves were likely American patriots and would be eager to help police arrest Russian communists. The brothers' talk and waving hands didn't last very long and then David came to front door and said, "Come back in the store, we've got something to say to you."

Parker reentered their store. David said, "Last March, we were questioned by Lieutenant Cambe of the Chicago police. He wanted us to locate Michael Klossmeier for him, which we did. I thought of Michael when I read about Oscar's murder because Michael's nickname was 'Mic the Knife' and the newspaper said Oscar's throat had been sliced with a knife. If I were an investigator, I would talk to Lieutenant Cambe and Michael Klossmeier about Oscar's death."

Parker thanked the brothers. Hearing 'Mic the Knife' mentioned was not a surprise but the implication that a Chicago Police Lieutenant who was Michael Boyle's boss may have been involved in Oscar's murder was a big and troubling surprise to Parker.

(35) Another Night at Gompers Park

On Friday, August 11, 1972, Parker and his son, Peter, returned to Gompers Park for another chess night. All the usual players were there including Jackson, Kyle, Lev, Frank Costello, and Barry Snyder. Peter was looking for Pavel Kotov, the player who had defeated Peter at a prior session because of Peter's unsound bishop sacrifice. He found Pavel who agreed to another game. The two started their game immediately, and after the opening moves, Parker walked away and left the main hall for the side rooms to talk to players who weren't playing serious chess but were socializing. There he saw Jackson, Frank, and Barry talking and joined the group.

Jackson asked Parker if he had heard anything about Bob Hanson. Parker shook his head no, and Jackson continued, "No one at Gompers Park has heard anything other than Bob did send a letter to the Club the first day he was in Reykjavik saying he had arrived and was looking forward to the World Championship Chess match."

"Perhaps he sent another letter commenting on the early games, but it hasn't yet arrived," offered Parker, "By the way, yesterday's game, the 13th game of the scheduled 24 games, was adjourned when Spassky sealed his 42nd move. What happened today when they resumed play?"

"Spassky resigned before the start of play, and thus, Fischer won a crazy remarkable game," said Barry. "The game probably should have been drawn but Spassky in some time pressure before the adjournment did not put his rook on the correct square. Fischer had a whole bunch of pawns and won when Spassky resigned on move 75. It was a fantastic game, the best thus far and the win really puts Fischer in control of the match."

"The commentators on TV are praising both players – Fischer wouldn't settle for a draw, kept finding ways to keep the pressure on, and turned in a win," commented Frank.

"So, Bobby takes the lead again by 3 game points, 8-5," summarized Parker.

"That's right," said Jackson, "it's the second time, he's up by 3 games. He was up by 3 games, 6.5 to 3.5, after winning game 10, but then he lost game 11."

"3 games up puts the pressure on Spassky to cut into the lead, otherwise Bobby can just play drawing lines and coast to winning the 24-round match," said Frank.

"Fischer is just proving again that's he's the best player in the world as ratings and consensus has been for some time," added Barry, "but this game 13 is remarkable – such an unbalanced position that Fischer manages to win. I'm going to be playing that game over for some time."

Fischer's game 13 win was clearly the big story for this night at Gompers Park, but another smaller story was unfolding for the Spooner family as Parker returned to his son's game and sat down to watch Peter play. This chess game went to a King and Pawn ending quickly and looked drawn. Pavel kept moving his King around trying to penetrate Peter's position, but Peter had been studying end games and kept opposition with his King so that Pavel's King could not enter Peter's territory. After repeating the same position three times, the chess game was officially drawn. Peter and Pavel shook hands. In the car on the way home, Peter was very excited about his play – he had held a very solid, experienced Class A player to a draw. “By the end of this year with more study, I think I should be able to start defeating players like Mr. Kotov,” said Peter. Parker was very happy for his enthusiastic son. He was learning the game by playing and improving.

Meanwhile, while all this was occurring at Gompers Park, that evening Father Joseph in his rectory was studying the life of Saint Clare of Assisi because August 11, was her feast day on the Church calendar. Father Joseph was preparing a short summary of Saint Clare’s life that he intended to distribute at the upcoming Sunday mass. His hope was that a person would hear the story of a saint’s life, relate to some facit of that life, and attempt to imitate it in the modern world.

Father Joseph wrote, As a young girl, Clare had dedicated herself to prayer. (Father Joseph wanted young people to pray.) After hearing Francis of Assisi preach during a Lenten service in the church of San Giorgio, she asked him to help her live according to the Gospel. (Father Joseph prayed that his sermons would bring people to live the Gospel.) Thus, on Palm Sunday in 1212, Clare left her father's home and went to the chapel of the Portiuncula to meet with Francis. This was a bold midnight escape from nobility in the upper areas of Assisi as she ran downward toward the lower city levels where Francis had established his Gospel mission among the poor. While there, Clare's hair was cut off, and she was given a plain robe and veil in exchange for her rich gown. This was a radical step for a young woman, and under the guidance of Francis, Clare joined the convent of the Benedictine nuns of San Paulo. Somewhere during this time, her father found her and attempted to force her to return home. She refused and professed that she would have no other husband than Jesus

Christ. (Father Joseph prayed that parents would not oppose their children from joining religious orders.)

Subsequently, Francis sent Clare to Sant' Angelo in Panzo, another Benedictine nuns' monastery because she desired greater solitude. Soon Clare's sister Catarina, who took the name Agnes, joined her. With the passage of time, other women joined them and a separate dwelling was built for them next to the church of San Damiano. All these women wanted to be brides of Jesus and live with no money. They became known as the Poor Ladies, living a life of austerity, seclusion, and poverty, according to a Rule which Francis gave them as a Second Order.

As the leader of her order, Clare defended them from clerical attempts to impose a rule that more closely followed the Rule of Saint Benedict rather than the rule given by Francis. Clare was completely devoted and dedicated to Francis and fought off every attempt from each pope trying to impose a rule on her order that would water down their "radical commitment to corporate poverty." (Father Joseph prayed that a religious order might grow according to God's will and not be snuffed out by a hostile hierarchy.)

In 1224, an army of soldiers from Frederick II came to attack Assisi. Although ill, Clare went out to meet them with the Blessed Sacrament in her hands. She had the Blessed Sacrament placed at the wall where the enemies could see it. Then on her knees, she begged God to save the Sisters. "O Lord, protect these Sisters whom I cannot protect now," she prayed. The attackers fled without harming anyone in Assisi. Clare is often pictured carrying a monstrance or pyx, to commemorate this time when she warded off the soldiers at the gates of her convent with the Blessed Sacrament.

Many times, before her death she expressed that no pain could trouble her. Her joy was in serving the Lord, and she once exclaimed: "They say that we are too poor, but can a heart which possesses the infinite God be truly called poor?"

After her death and canonization, the construction of the Basilica of Saint Clare was finished in 1260, and her remains transferred there. The Order of Poor Ladies was officially changed to the Order of Saint Clare in 1263 by Pope Urban IV.

St. Clare was designated as the patron saint of television in 1958 by Pope Pius XII, because when St. Clare was very ill, she could not attend mass and was reportedly able to see and hear it on the wall in her room. She is also the patroness of eye disease, goldsmiths, and laundry.

Father Joseph learned many things about St. Clare by reading about her that August 11th night in 1972. St. Clare was just one saint of many, and Father Joseph prayed for more saints and that their life stories would become known in the future. "Lord," prayed Father Joseph, "we give thanks for the Saints, such as St. Clare, because it's through them that we see You."

The next day, Saturday, Father Joseph typed the summary of St. Clare's life on a piece of paper. His rectory had a photocopier, and he made copies of what he had typed, and the next day, Sunday, the life of St. Clare was distributed to parishioners at mass. The Spooner family received a copy. Parker read it to his family at Sunday dinner. After dinner, he folded the piece of paper and placed it in his pocket.

(36) Delia Has Breast Cancer

Late Sunday afternoon, Marsha telephoned Parker and said she had switched the knives and would be back in Chicago that night, and since she wasn't scheduled to work at the restaurant on Monday morning, perhaps that would be a good time to give the knife to the police. Parker said he could meet her early Monday morning at her house and take Marsha to the police station, where she would give Sergeant Boyle the knife and make a statement. Marsha quickly took him up on the offer. The thought that the knife she now had in her possession was the actual knife that killed Oscar was troubling to Marsha. She wanted to give the weapon to the police as quickly as possible. Parker set a time to meet her and then called his father-in-law to alert him that he might be getting the actual murder weapon Monday morning. The Sergeant, of course, was happy to hear this news.

That night as he tried to fall asleep, Parker kept mulling over various possibilities as to who was responsible for Oscar's murder and how the crime had actually occurred. In his mind, Parker lined up all the facts regarding Oscar's murder and then started thinking about them. He couldn't really do all of this mentally, and thus quietly slipped out of bed, went to his desk, turned on his nightlight, and began writing.

"Is everything okay, Parker?" said Rosemary from the bed. He had tried to be quiet, but after 22 years of marriage, she knew he was no longer next to her side.

"Yes, all is good, darling. I couldn't fall asleep and kept thinking about Oscar's murder and various possibilities.

I'm just writing everything down, so I don't forget anything in the morning."

"That's great news, Parker. In the middle of the night, you might solve your case! Perhaps we should celebrate when you return to the bed."

"Sounds good to me, my love. I'll definitely speed up my writing," he said with a big smile on his face.

The following morning Parker went to Marsha's house to take her to the police station. She had carefully wrapped the knife she had confiscated from Mic and held it tightly, but her face revealed that she had been crying and was distraught, "My mother told me this morning that she has breast cancer. I can't believe it; she's only 45 years old."

"I'm sorry to hear that. How did Delia find out that she has breast cancer?" inquired Parker.

"She went to her doctor, who said her mammogram had tested positive."

"Okay that's the result of one test. It doesn't mean that she actually has breast cancer," replied Parker.

"Her doctor says it's 90% certain that she has breast cancer."

Parker shook his head no – that couldn't possibly be right. He had to clarify the situation for Marsha, who was upset. "I don't think that 90% certain can be the correct number based on only one mammogram. Is that the actual situation for your mother? Was this her first and only mammogram?"

"Yes, she never had a mammogram before."

"Ok, so I'm back to my original statement. One positive test can't equate to being 90% *certain* of cancer. After you're finished talking to the police and given them Mic's knife, perhaps you could do some research in a medical library gathering some facts, and then I'd help you calculate the real chance of cancer given one mammogram indicating that something maybe wrong."

"What would I be looking for in the medical library?" asked Marsha.

"Well first of all, you would find out the probability that a woman of your mother's age actually has breast cancer."

"Okay, I'm certain that the librarian at my night school could find that statistic. My mother is age 45."

"Then ask the librarian if she can find the statistic that if a *woman has breast cancer*, what's the chance of a positive mammogram."

"Let me write this down," said Marsha, "these statistics sound like what I'm learning in my night school statistic's class." Marsha had a small notebook in her skirt pocket and started writing.

"Finally," said Parker, "find the statistic that if *a woman does not have breast cancer*, what's the chance of a false positive mammogram."

"Okay, I'll give it a shot. What happens if I find these probabilities?'

"Give me a call, and I'll come over and we'll give your mother, Delia, the correct estimate that she has breast cancer based on one positive test. I'm confident that's it nowhere close to 90%"

Marsha looked at Parker – her tears had disappeared and now hope showed in her eyes. "How do you know all this stuff?" she asked.

"I went to a good college, paid attention, and did homework which required learning some math," replied a smiling Parker.

He then reached into his pocket and took out the folded piece of paper that summarized St. Clare's life. "It's also helpful to read about canonized saints. I think your mother might find reading about St. Clare of Assisi helpful. Her feast day was last Friday, and this brief description of her life was handed out after mass yesterday by Father Joseph."

Marsha took the paper, "Thank you, Parker, I'll give it to my mother. She has been telling me for some time that we should start going to Sunday mass. This may encourage her to actually start." Marsha could not know it, but she had just made a perceptive statement. The brief summary of St. Clare's life that Father Joseph had written would have a positive impact on Delia.

They arrived at the police station, and Marsha gave the knife to Sergeant Boyle who passed it to Detective Brendan. Parker hadn't talked recently about Oscar's murder with his father-in-law, and thus the two of them went into a side room, while Detective Brendan took Marsha's statement about how she had switched knives while Mic was sleeping, and thus the police now had Mic's knife, which they would be testing for blood samples and the cuts it made.

"We haven't talked in some time," said Sergeant Boyle "and the latest is that the Fort Lauderdale police apprehended Susan Delford last week, and she's being extradited back here tomorrow, Tuesday morning. Later that afternoon, we'll be questioning her about her activity the night Oscar was murdered and her whereabouts the last few weeks. I don't know if you're interested in joining us but you may since you were involved with her initial interview."

Parker hadn't heard from Susan since their phone conversation. She was supposed to move to Fort Lauderdale, stay with one of her friends, and call Parker when she got there. Now Parker understood why she hadn't called. The police in Florida had detained her as a suspect in Oscar's murder. Parker promised Aurelia that he would not involve the Chicago police in their CIA investigation, but he wasn't doing that here. It was the police, his father-in-law, who were involving him. Thus, Parker explained to his father-in-law that Susan had contacted him and explained how she had seen Oscar the night of the murder and that he gave her his current black book which was similar to prior ones except for the word anagram. Parker then explained how Susan located Boris Vulkov and what Boris was doing along the Miami docks.

The Sergeant was surprised by these facts and then he and Parker discussed possible implications as to how Oscar's murder went down and who had ordered the murder. The Sergeant had to sit down as he thought about some of the scenarios that Parker had constructed the night before. After reflecting, the Sergeant decided to change his planned upcoming action in the scheduled meeting with Susan Danford. Even though Oscar's murder was not yet fully understood, the Sergeant knew that there was absolutely no reason to hold Miss Danford based on what Parker had conveyed.

Thus, the next afternoon, Sergeant Boyle and Detective Brendan met Susan Danford, who had been extradited from Florida. "We're releasing you but *do not run away again*," said the Sergeant to Susan. "We know that you saw Oscar the night he was murdered and that he gave you his black book that night. He also told you not to trust the police because the police were corrupt. That was why, during our initial interview, you didn't acknowledge being in Oscar's apartment the night of the murder and then didn't tell us that Oscar gave you his black book, which you subsequently mailed to Parker. I understand all of that *now* but just remember that *this Homicide Unit is not corrupt*, Miss Danford, and we *will find Oscar's murderer*. For now, you are to lie low, talk to no one, but be available if we have further questions. Do you understand all of what I've just conveyed?"

Susan was surprised but recognized Parker's influence in what just happened, and of course, she was delighted at this development and had to contain her impulse to jump up and kiss the *incorrupt* police, both Sergeant Boyle and Detective Brendan. Instead, she contained her urges and merely replied, "Yes, sir, what you said is true, and I'm truly relieved to hear this, and I promise that I shall not talk to anyone about this case and will be available to answer any further questions that you may have. Thank you for releasing me!"

(37) Delia

When Delia read the words that Father Joseph had written about St. Clare of Assisi, she was moved because she recognized certain virtues and attributes in St. Clare's life that centuries later had helped Delia herself in her own life.

Growing up near the Chicago Stock Yards Delia married John Dempsey right out of high school because the young man could not wait, and Delia would not engage in sexual intercourse without a marriage. Marsha was born a year later, and the couple, using money from his parents, bought a modest house near the stock yards. John could not handle marriage, a child, and a house and ran away to California when Marsha started grammar school. His parents were appalled and paid off the house, making Delia the sole owner, and left her a small amount of money before they followed their son to California.

Delia worked as a waitress at a nearby restaurant. She would walk Marsha to school every morning, go to work, and pick Marsha up from school at the end of a school day. Delia was part of a network of women that collectively worked together to juggle kids, work, and in some cases husbands. Delia was smart and industrious and lived a full life in the south side neighborhood where everyone knew her. In high school, Marsha did well, got excellent grades, but was recognized as an independent person who did not join any particular group of students. Jim Leaver was the guy who lived in the neighborhood and her partner at all the school dances. Delia watched Marsha grow to maturity and said many silent prayers for her daughter.

Reading and thinking about St. Clare, allowed Delia to relate her life to Clare's life in modest and various ways.

First, when Delia was pregnant, she had *dedicated* herself to the baby growing inside of her, and thus she understood Clare's *dedication* to prayer as described by Father Joseph. Second, Clare received help from Francis of Assisi, and Delia received help from the parents of her husband, and thus the *virtue of receiving and accepting help* was important to both women even though they were separated by centuries and different societies.

Moreover, Clare was the leader of an order of religious women while Delia had been part of a group of like-minded neighborhood women who helped each other and where Delia was one of the leaders. Clare had saved her order by praying to God and standing up in front of invaders while Delia experienced countless times where she had to protect herself, her child, and their home from daily struggles and setbacks.

The fact that all of this was becoming clearer to Delia at age 45 was a blessing, and she gave thanks to the hidden God who was now very much in focus for her.

(38) Parker Uses Bayesian Statistical Methods

Marsha search in the medical library found that there was a 0.8% probability that a 40-to-50-year-old woman has breast cancer.

She then discovered that any woman having breast cancer had a 90% probability of receiving a positive mammogram. That was the reverse statement of her mother's situation! Delia had a positive mammogram and was now asking for the probability of cancer, not the other way around. Her doctor, who had conveyed a 90% chance of breast cancer to Delia, had reversed the statements and his estimate of 90% was going to be incorrect.

A more difficult search, but the medical librarian was very helpful here and found that a woman without breast cancer would 7% of the time receive a false positive mammogram. Marsha, looking at her textbook, knew she had all the information necessary to tell her mother, Delia, the actual probability that she had breast cancer.

Marsha called Parker with her findings and invited him to stop by their house to talk to Delia about her positive mammogram, which he did one evening. Delia greeted Parker warmly, and the three sat around the kitchen table. Delia had baked pastries and Parker joined the ladies eating and drinking tea.

"My daughter says that her textbook has a statistical method that shows a 90% chance of breast cancer for me is pure hogwash," said a smiling Delia directly addressing Parker.

"Yes, Mrs. Demsey, Marsha has gathered statistics that we can use to estimate the probability that you actually have breast council based on one positive mammogram."

"Marsha has been explaining the numbers to me, but I find it confusing. Perhaps I could have your perspective."

"Yes, Mrs. Demsey, we are going to be using Bayesian statistics to estimate the probability that you have breast cancer."

"Please call me Delia – Mrs. Demsey sounds too old, and I'll call you Parker."

"Very good," said a smiling Parker, "Bayesian statistics date from 1763 when Richard Price, a mathematician, presented a paper written by his late friend, the Reverend Thomas Bayes, to the British Royal Society. At the heart of Bayesian thought is the notion that probabilities represent *degrees of belief about uncertain statements*."

"Perhaps," said Marsha, "you could give us examples of uncertain statements."

Parker quickly rattled off:

"Richard Nixon will be reelected President this November; the Oakland Athletics will win the World Series this October; the coin I'm tossing has a true probability of heads between 0.498 and 0.502. All three of these statements are uncertain. No one knows if Nixon will be reelected, no one knows if Oakland will win the World Series, no one knows if the coin being flipped is weighted or not." Both Delia and Marsha were nodding agreement that those statements were uncertain. Parker then continued, "the basic idea of Bayesian inference is that uncertain statements are continually updated in light of empirical data. In your case Delia we have the statement that there is a 0.8% probability that a 40-to-50-year-old woman has breast cancer. That applies to you Delia because you are a woman in that age group. Now we are going to update that estimate because you have a positive mammogram."

"Okay, and when you do that what is the updated number?" asked Delia.

"When I did the calculation, I got that .008 was updated to .094," said Marsha. Parker nodded in agreement.

"That's a 9.4% chance of breast cancer – nowhere close to the 90% that the doctor told me," said a pleased Delia.

"Yes, and now if we could find another independent factor that goes into breast cancer, we could update the 9.4%. No single piece of evidence is decisive in a Bayesian analysis rather each piece of evidence goes into updating the probability that the patient has cancer."

"Anyway, I can't tell you the relief I feel that based on one positive mammogram the chance of cancer is 9%, not 90%. Thank you, Parker, and Marsha I'm really proud of you – you stayed in school and now I'm starting to see the results of the bright girl I always knew you were."

Marsha smiled at her mother and a slight red blush showed on her face.

"May I look at that piece of paper that shows the calculation as to how .008 became .094," said Delia.

"Sure, mother, here it is. Pr is short for probability," replied Marsha displaying a paper that read:

Prior probability: Pr(cancer) = .008

True positive rate: Pr(positive | cancer) = .90

False positive rate: Pr(positive | no cancer) = .07

Pr(cancer | positive) = [.90*.008] /{[.90*.008]+[.07*.992]}
= .0072 / (.0072 + .06944) = .094

"It's that last long equation that's confusing to me - the probability that I have cancer given a positive mammogram. I can do the arithmetic given the numbers shown and obtain 9.4% but where does that formula come from?" said Delia.

"Mother, I don't think I understand the book's explanation. I just wrote the formula down from the textbook and used it."

With that the two women looked at Parker, who said "The doctor told you 90% because the probability of having a positive test given that you have breast cancer is 90%. However, that's not what you wanted to know. You wanted the reverse of that. You wanted the probability of having cancer given that you tested positive. Those two statements *are not equal.*" Parker then wrote: Pr(cancer | positive) **does not equal** Pr (positive | cancer) = which does equal .90"

Both Delia and Marsha nodded yes to wanting to know the probability of cancer given a positive test. Parker continued talking and writing on a piece of paper, "Now mathematically, the probability of having cancer given a positive test can be written:

Pr(positive | cancer)Pr(cancer)/Pr(positive) or substituting then for Pr(positive) yields

$Pr(positive|cancer)Pr(cancer)/[Pr(positive|cancer)Pr(cancer) + Pr(positive|nocancer)Pr(nocancer)]$

If you look at that last equation, you see its form is A/(A+B) where A is testing positive for cancer given that you have it and B is testing positive for cancer when you don't have it. Now A+B is the total; you either have cancer, or you don't have cancer. Thus, A/(A+B) gives us the percentage that has tested positive and has the disease, and that percentage is 9.4% after you have done the arithmetic."

Both Delia and Marsha were smiling now. The 9% chance that Delia had cancer made more sense than the Doctor's 90% because the cancer diagnosis was based only on one test. They thanked Parker for taking the time to explain this to them.

Delia thanked Parker for the paper on St. Clare. Parker's kindness greatly impressed them. Because both Marsha's and Delia's confidence in the way that things were structured in the world was increased, they started to change the way they lived their lives. Marsha vowed to stop dating men who were interested only in themselves. Delia put all her affairs into order just in case she was seriously ill and had a second mammogram, which showed everything was normal.

Shortly thereafter, Delia accompanied by Marsha started attending Sunday mass and heard Father Joseph talk. Father Joseph said he learned a prayer for healing by studying Padre Pio, who had died in September 1968. Padre Pio was widely regarded as a holy priest and a likely future saint. Here was his prayer:

"Heavenly Father, I thank you for loving me. I thank you for sending your Son, Our Lord Jesus Christ, to the world to save and to set me free. I trust in your power and grace that sustain and restore me. Loving Father, touch me now with your healing hands, for I believe that your will is for me to be well in mind, body, soul and spirit. Cover me with the most precious blood of your Son, our Lord Jesus Christ from the top of my head to the soles of my feet. Cast anything that should not be in me. Root out any unhealthy and abnormal cells. Open any blocked arteries or veins and rebuild and replenish any damaged areas. Remove all inflammation and cleanse any infection by the power of Jesus' precious blood. Let the fire of your healing love pass through my entire body to heal and make new any diseased areas so that my body will function the way you created it to function. Touch also my mind and my emotion, even the deepest recesses of my heart. Saturate my entire being with your presence, love, joy, and peace and draw me ever closer to you every moment of my life. And Father, fill me with your Holy Spirit and empower me to do your works so that my life will bring glory and honor to your holy name. I ask this in the name of the Lord Jesus Christ. Amen."

Delia and Marsha were deeply moved by this prayer. They found the words shocking and the imagery that was conveyed resonated with them. "We'll be going to Church every Sunday from now on," vowed both of them after reflecting on Padre Pio's words.

(39) Aurelia and Dmitry at Dinner

Dmitry invited Aurelia to have dinner with him at a small restaurant in the heart of Miami. She accepted. They ordered - Dmitry a steak and mashed potatoes and Aurelia chicken and French fries. Both would be drinking coffee. While they waited, Dmitry started talking, “What I would like to do is have a truce between us. We’re both trying to do something that could impact humanity in a positive way. We’re trying to convey information between humans and dolphins. That’s more important than the current tension between the United States and the Soviet Union. If humans are able to understand the workings of the cetacean brain and start communicating with dolphins, then this breakthrough might bring the two nations and species together for the benefit of all.”

“A noble sentiment but how in practice could this be achieved?” asked Aurelia.

“I think we’re both making progress in our work with dolphins. We’ve both started basic communication with them. We have both recorded their whistles and chirps. It’s likely both nations will use dolphins as spies once effective communication begins. My hope is that I can guide my group into actually communicating with the dolphins to learn more about how nature works in the oceans and that dolphins are not weaponized by humans,” said Dmitry.

“Unfortunately, if dolphins could be trained to spy and if you’re communicating with them, then they would convey to you whatever they discovered during their spying,” answered Aurelia.

"I'm hoping that they have an inner life like humans, and we're able to reach them in that capacity and not use them as spies," said Dmitry.

"Sadly, we humans have an inner life, but we spy on each other and have terrible wars. We're likely to pass that along to dolphins if they're not that way already," said Aurelia.

Dmitry looked at Aurelia and confessed, "I think I'm finally becoming religious, Aurelia. Mankind with our wars shows that we're a fallen species. I hope the dolphins are innocent and are able to avoid our wars."

At that moment the waiter brought out food, and they briefly stopped talking while the waiter served them, "Would either of you like anything else at this moment?" asked the waiter.

"Nothing for me, thank you," said Aurelia, while Dmitry looked at the waiter and shook his head no. With that they started eating and then Aurelia continued by commenting on Dmitry's last point, "There is nothing wrong with becoming religious, Dmitry. Creation has an order to it, and it's rational to acknowledge the obvious. With respect to dolphins, have you seen any indication that they have an inner life similar to a human?"

"Not yet, but we're only just getting started. It's like we have only a few words right now, and it's all perception stuff. How about you, Aurelia?"

"Yes, it's the same for us. It's exactly like communicating with apes, and I don't expect our attempts to get to conceptional ideas will work with dolphins, just as it hasn't worked with apes."

"I'm glad we're talking about this, Aurelia," responded Dmitry.

Aurelia didn't say anything but continued eating.

Dmitry continued talking, "I would like to meet on a regular basis to see if either of us are experiencing any changes or progress. Aurelia, would you be willing to meet once a week for supper or lunch to talk about dolphins?"

"That's sounds good to me, Dmitry. Let's do these updates over lunch." Aurelia said this because lunch would be a shorter period of time than dinner, and she would have to get back to work, which would naturally cut off longer and complicated discussions. Furthermore, dinner could lead to late hours and other activities. Aurelia realized that she *cared for* Dmitry even though he was very naïve by continuing to be involved with soviet spies. Aurelia knew herself, and she had to watch her feelings for him. Additionally, she knew Dmitry likely fantasized about her as a woman in his inner life, and if she gave any indication that she liked him, he would be all over her.

And thus, it happened that Aurelia and Dmitry began seeing each other once a week for lunch. They talked about communicating with dolphins. Dmitry and Boris had already identified two dolphins, which they named Alpha and Beta, because these two seemed to grasp English commands better than the other dolphins. Sometimes Alpha and Beta didn't appear when Boris was out on the ocean in his boat, holding his microphone and recording their whistles and clicks; however, whenever he spotted either Alpha or Beta, he would switch to his second tape recorder, which played a prerecorded tape of instructions that Dmitry had made. Boris played this tape loudly so that all the dolphins could listen to what Dmitry was asking them to do. Generally, progress was made whenever Alpha or Beta were there to listen to Dmitry's tape because they responded.

Aurelia, in turn, indicated that Jenkins apparently was doing similar work with a new agent that recently had come on board. "I've never met this new agent because Jenkins deals with him directly. We just call him agent D because he's the fourth agent in our unit behind Williams, Stein, and Watts. Right now, he's apparently dealing with cetacean communication which includes whales and seals besides dolphins," said Aurelia to Dmitry.

Meanwhile, more and more Aurelia was aware that she cared for Dmitry and that if he ever attempted to kiss her then she would find it awkward to respond in a negative manner, but she wouldn't allow him to kiss her on her lips as lovers do because she was in love with Frank Jenkins. What she felt about Dmitry was that his quest for knowledge was admirable. Yes, he was tall, good-looking, and intelligent and all of that helped her growing admiration of him, yet she also knew his weakness, which was a political nativity about communism that prevented him from seeing that it wasn't working in the Soviet Union or anywhere else, and in many situations, it was oppressive and evil. However, his drive to understand dolphins, their whistles and clicks and their possible inner life, was a positive human force similar to what had inspired other individuals to discover things about reality that had escaped the notice of everyone else. It was the same force that had driven other individuals to discover human, religious, and scientific truths, and because of this internal drive within

Dmitry, Aurelia was in that sense in love with that aspect of him.

As time passed, Aurelia finally came to realize that her love for Dmitry wasn't really a woman falling in love with a man, but it was more like a mother watching her wayward offspring and hoping that he would be able to successively navigate a dangerous world. He, in turn, began to respond to her like a son who needed help. She had made it clear to him that there would be no romance between them, but she cared for him, and he, like a son, accepted that and looked for guidance from her.

At the same time, Aurelia realized that this situation could not continue. It would come to an end one way or another. As a woman, the man she loved and desired was Frank Jenkins. She was certain that Frank cared for her but because he was fifteen years older than her and was her boss, he would never act in an inappropriate or romantic manner. Now Frank had evidence that both Dmitry and Boris were Soviet spies, and papers for their arrest were complete and would be served soon. A day of reckoning was quickly approaching, and Aurelia had to decide what she was going to do about her wayward "son", Dmitry.

(40) Parker Sees the Light

Parker Spooner had finally figured out who was responsible for Oscar's murder. He had done it by initially writing facts down on individual pieces of paper. Thus he had dozens of pieces of paper including the names of everyone involved - some folks in Chicago, others in Florida – along with dates of events, but the most critical pieces of paper were Oscar's last black book with ANAGRAM written on the back cover and the LOOK TO COLLECT ALL MONEY BY ELEVEN note. At that moment, he saw what Oscar had done and had figured out Oscar's last message. But now he had the difficult task of conveying what he discovered to Sergeant Michael Boyle. He called his father-in-law and said he was coming to the police station to talk to him about the murderer. The Sergeant was surprised, "Great, I'll be waiting for you, son-in-law."

Once there, Parker started the conversation slowly with his father-in-law, "Dad, we haven't talked in some time because I've been busy working on Oscar's death, but now I must raise a sensitive issue with you since that case involves the Chicago police department and your immediate boss, Lieutenant Gary Camby."

"I'm listening, Parker, go ahead and raise your issue," replied a surprised Sergeant Boyle.

"Here's Oscar Busby's latest black book where he kept a record of his bets," said Parker waving the black book.

The Sergeant took the book, thumbed through it, and saw the word 'anagram" printed on the back cover in capital letters. "Okay," he said, "you've gone through this book, figured something out and now you're here, telling me what it means. Please continue."

“When you first came to me about Oscar’s murder, you came with a sheet of paper that had the start of a mortality table on the back, which was quite appropriate to show it to me since I’m a life insurance actuary, but what else was on the front side of that paper?”

“A handwritten message in capital letters about an eleven o’clock meeting,” said Sergeant Boyle.

“Yes,” said Parker, “and specifically the message read, ‘LOOK TO COLLECT ALL MONEY BY ELEVEN’. That message wasn’t written by the killer. It was written by Oscar an hour before his murder on a piece of paper that came from the Murray’s basement. Now Oscar writes not only that message but prints the word ‘ANAGRAM’ on his black book which he gives to Susan right before his murder.” Parker pauses.

“I’m with you – please continue,” said the Sergeant leaning forward because he recognized that Parker was getting close to revealing Oscar’s killer.

“Thus, if the message LOOK TO COLLECT ALL MONEY BY ELEVEN is an *anagram* written by Oscar before his murder, then we have L T C A M B E. Oscar, who loved codes and writing abbreviated messages in his black book, has with this anagram named his spy and the man who ordered his murder!”

When he heard this, Sergeant Boyle physically jumped out of his chair, “Lieutenant Cambe! Parker, you can’t be serious; those letters are just a coincidence. I don’t know if I should laugh or cry at this! Are you actually saying Lieutenant Cambe is the Soviet spy that Oscar found?”

"Yes, it appears that way, Cambe is a Soviet spy. He realizes Oscar is on to him and hires this guy Michael Klossmeier to kill Oscar. When I questioned the Glueck brothers, they said they gave Klossmeier or Mic the Knife's address to the Lieutenant during a police interview because Cambe wanted it."

"Okay, so Cambe had Mic the knife's address. That doesn't prove that Cambe contacted Mic or hired him to murder Oscar." Sergeant Boyle remained skeptical. He didn't like Camby but the notion that the Lieutenant was actually a Soviet agent seemed ridiculous to him. Boyle continued, "Lieutenant Camby is sometimes difficult to figure out, but Camby as a Russian spy seems over the top. Really Parker, what's the basis for this accusation besides the anagram message, LOOK TO COLLECT ALL MONEY BY ELEVEN?"

"Mic's come into a lot of money recently and is now buying a house in Madison, Wisconsin. The money is his payoff for the murder. We can attempt to find out where the money Mic is receiving is coming from. It's likely from a Swiss bank account owned by the Soviets. By the way, you recall Lieutenant Cambe kicked up a big fuss when the CIA came directly to you, the Homicide Unit responsible for solving Oscar's murder, rather than going through him. Cambe wanted everything to go through him. That could be respect for the chain of command or an opportunity to deflect any potential evidence that would implicate him. Anyway, thanks to Marsha, who replaced Mic's knife with another knife, you likely have the murder weapon. If Mic's knife shows any of Oscar's blood on it or if the striations on the knife match the cut marks on Oscar's throat, then you'll have evidence to arrest him."

"This is very serious if any of it has any truth. All the stuff that the CIA gave to us has been sent to Lieutenant Cambe because he requested it," said the Sergeant.

"Jenkins gave us the names of nine individuals who might be spies. Cambe would certainly be interested in that information, especially if he's a spy himself. Of course, he's probably laughing if every spy he knows is missing from the list." Parker paused and allowed the Sergeant to reflect on all of this before continuing, "I'm not certain how you're going to handle this, Dad, but I'll be contacting Aurelia at the CIA."

"Okay, Parker, that makes sense to me. Thanks for calling this surprising possibility to my attention, and I'll certainly be considering it before I make any further decisions regarding Oscar's murder. In the meantime, please be careful, son-in-law."

Wow, Gary Cambe, a Russian spy! That could explain the Lieutenant's miserable attitude, thought Sergeant Boyle, but he didn't say that to Parker.

(41) Aurelia Digs Deeper

As Aurelia was struggling with the proper way of handling Dmitry Doby and her maternal feelings for him, the telephone rang, and Parker was on the line.

Parker made the case to Aurelia that Oscar knew Lieutenant Cambe was a Soviet spy and was seeking that evidence when Oscar was murdered. Aurelia agreed that the word anagram on Oscar's last black book and the message LOOK TO COLLECT ALL MONEY BY ELEVEN was not a coincidence but a deliberate action by Oscar who was worried for his own safety. She thought that Oscar had named in a coded message the Soviet spy and the man who hired his killer and that was LT CAMBE. It made sense to her because using a code like that was part of Oscar's style.

Aurelia then dug deeper into CIA files. They already had a file on Barry Snyder as a likely soviet courier. Barry was a brother-in-law to the Lieutenant as both the men had married Kotov sisters. CIA investigators found that Cambe's rise in the Chicago Police Department was all warranted. He was an excellent police officer and had received several commendations and two awards from the Department for outstanding work. He even went to night school and earned a college degree. He was an only child and had married early, right after high school to a girl he had started dating when they were juniors. Mrs. Cambe was a grammar school teacher, and they had no children. "Thus far, we aren't finding anything detrimental in Cambe's background," said Aurelia in a subsequent phone call to Parker.

"What about the Lieutenant's wife and her family?" asked Parker.

"Cambe's wife is a woman named Vera Kotov. Her family emigrated from Russia during the 1920's."

"Okay," said Parker, "so there's the Russian connection."

"But apparently this family was trying to flee the Bolshevik Revolution."

"Russians didn't agree on their revolution but murdering the Czar and his family got rid of the aristocrats and nobles and set the country on a path toward communism. It would be interesting to investigate if there were other Cambe relatives who came to America besides the Kotov family. I know a chess player at the Gompers Park Chess Club whose last name is Kotov. Let me do some digging there." Here, Parker was thinking about Pavel Kotov, Peter's recent chess opponent at Gompers Park.

"Okay, and I'll also dig deeper into the Kotov name. After all, that was your insight, wasn't it? – that the two of us together would solve Oscar's murder," said a smiling Aurelia.

"Yes, together we'll solve a murder and also reveal some secret," added Parker.

With Parker's mention of a secret, Aurelia stopped smiling and became nervous. She thought about the CIA secret regarding dolphins, but now she was wondering if Parker's insight might be related to her recently developed secret, which was that she had become emotionally attached, not as a lover, but as a mother figure to Dmitry Doby. "I'll get back to you as soon as I learn anything," said Aurelia as she hung up the phone and went into a long think.

Finally, it became clear to her what she had to do, and she called Dmitry on the phone. "I want you to come to my apartment tonight to talk. This is not about romance or sex so get that out of your mind. You're in trouble and both of us know it, and we need a frank discussion."

"I can be there around 8:00 o'clock," said Dmitry with a bit of surprise in his voice.

"That's good, and by the way, do not tell any of your comrades about this talk and come by yourself," said Aurelia. With that she went to her hidden tape recorder and made certain it was functioning properly; she tested that it was picking up words that she spoke softly. The conversation that she was about to have with Dmitry was definitely one conversation that she wanted to record even if they started whispering.

When Dmitry arrived, he found Miss Qundo reading an encyclopedia. "Here's what's written about dolphins," she said. "Because of their intelligence and their ability to communicate with one another through a range of distorted sounds, dolphins have been the object of serious scientific experimentation." With that, she laughed out loud and closed the book. "Based on what you and I know that seems to be quite an understatement," continued Aurelia looking directly at Dmitry Doby.

"Yes," he replied, "textbooks have a way of being out of date even before they are written."

"But don't you think it's much better that the public is unaware of the true abilities of dolphins?" said Aurelia. "If they learned of a society structured by sea mammals, cultural shock and repercussions might be enormous and unpredictable. It's much better to do what the United States does and deflect public thoughts of aliens as gray creatures in flying saucers living far away in outer space rather than the highly intelligent life living in our oceans."

"I suppose you're correct, but what disturbs me," replied Dmitry with a sudden change in the tone of his voice as he moved very close to Aurelia "is the murder of Gorky Genkin. I think your agent D killed him. I wonder about the identity of Agent D? Who is he, and what does he know about our operation?"

Aurelia pulled away from him. "Dmitry, I've been trying to find the identity of D. No one knows except Jenkins. I believe Jenkins and D meet at the abandoned warehouse on the Intracoastal Waterway, but Jenkins writes nothing down and keeps everything in his head. No one can get close to him – his reticent nature is legendary throughout the Agency. I have tried … believe me … I have tried. I thought I could get his attention, but Jenkins remains oblivious, completely focused on his work."

What Aurelia said was true, but she didn't want to talk about Frank afraid that she might accidentally reveal in some manner that she was in love with him. However, what she had just said to Dmitry was essentially the truth. She did not know the identity of Agent D, other than he was closely related to the dolphin project that the CIA was directing. Indeed, apparently Agent D had identified the various dolphin pods in the Atlantic Ocean off of Florida and had named them. The dolphins were an amazing species, and the CIA was determined to use them to protect the United States if they could be trained to offer such protection.

"Aurelia, I realize that you have been making attempts, but something different needs to happen. I think both Boris and I are in danger. At any moment, we may be completely shut down and arrested.” He was genuinely frightened that the worst was about to happen.

Miss Qundo looked directly into his eyes. “Do not worry Dmitry. I will warn you before anything like that happens. The assignments given to arresting agents pass across my desk a day in advance. You will have time to clear out if anything like that happens. Besides, the person that advises you would probably alert you to anything in advance, wouldn’t he do that?”

“Yes, I believe he would, but I don’t know if Sergei has any way of knowing what the CIA is doing. Anyway, I’m fortunate to have you working in Jenkins’ office.” With that, Dmitry Doby gave Aurelia Qundo a hug, and she smiled, having learned the first name of his contact. She would now talk to Parker.

(42) Parker Talks to Pavel

After making an appointment on the phone, Parker went to Pavel Kotov's apartment on the north side of Chicago near Gompers Park. Pavel was waiting and ushered him into a small, three-room apartment that had a chess board set up in the living room where most folks had their television. Besides a sofa and a side table with a lamp, the living room had two large completely full bookcases and about half the books and magazines were related to chess, divided fairly evenly among chess openings, middle games, and endings.

"I have my TV in the bedroom, and I watch the 10:00 evening news in bed before retiring," said Pavel. "Right now, I'm going to get myself something to drink – may I get you a beer, soda, tea, or coffee?"

"Nothing, for me, thank you," responded Parker as he sat down on the sofa.

Pavel returned holding a can of Miller's for himself and took a seat next to Parker, "Your young son, Peter, is a very good chess player for someone his age. I expect he will be passing me in ratings very soon. It's also fun to play someone young who you know is going to be a very good chess player soon. You never can tell if the kid will develop into a grandmaster and then you can show off your win against him when he was just starting out." Pavel smiled broadly at this pleasant thought before continuing. "Anyway, you said on the phone you wanted to talk to me about my family name, Kotov, since you've come across it in one of your investigations."

"Yes, that's correct. I would appreciate you telling me about as many Kotov relatives that you're aware of."

“Well, there’s not too many of us. I was one of three children – two boys and a girl. I never married. My brother, Emil, did, and he and his wife had two girls and both of the girls married and had children, but none of them carry the Kotov last name. My sister, Anna, married and had a bunch of kids, six to be exact, but none of them carry the Kotov last name. However, when my Dad came to the United States, he arrived with two of his brothers and they married and there are Kotov’s from those marriages.”

“I wonder if you could share with me some of those Kotov’s first names?”

“Well, let me think – there’s Anatoly, Sofia, Ludmila, Denis and Sergei. That’s it, five Kotov’s from my uncles.”

“Would you be able to tell me something about each one of your cousins?”

“I haven’t seen most of them in a long time. Uncle Rafik had three children. Anatoly was a lithographer, and I saw him on his 25th wedding anniversary. I lost contact with Sofia. I was at Ludmila’s wedding, and she and her family live here in Chicago, and I do see them from time to time. She sends me a Christmas card every year. On the other side, Denis and Sergei are sons of Uncle Vladimir, and I haven’t seen either of them in years. Denis left for California many years ago. Sergei was a rough kid, and my parents said he was always up to no good. I have no idea where he is or what he’s doing.”

“I wonder if you know a Vera Kotov?” asked Parker.

“Yes, Vera is one of my cousins. My brother Emil had two girls. Vera was one of them. I was at her wedding years ago, but we've never really kept in touch with each other. She married a cop, but I can't recall his name right now."

"Gary Cambe," prompted Parker.

"Yes, that's it! You're up on my family tree," replied Pavel with a smile, "She's been a Vera Cambe for some time now."

"Do they have any children?"

"No."

"Besides Vera, your brother Emil had another child."

"Yea, that's Veronica. She married Barry Snyder, my chess player friend from Gompers Park, a long time ago and has children but all of them carry the Snyder last name."

"Okay, if I need any more information about your sister Anna's six children, I'll contact you, but I think that covers it. If you think of something additional, please let me know the next time I see you at the chess club, but to summarize, I believe it's fair to conclude that you don't have many contacts with Kotov descendants."

"That's correct – other than my brother Emil and sister Anna, I seldom see their families. All my friends are neighbors, people I worked with before retirement, and chess players at Gompers Park."

Parker was satisfied and walked away with the following chart of Pavel Kotov's family in his head:

Pavel's Father
(m. 3 children)

Pavel Kotov
(not married)

Emil Kotov
(m. 2 girls)

Anna Kotov
(m. 6 children)

Vera Kotov m.
Gary Cambe, no kids
Veronica Kotov m.
Barry Snyder, kids

Uncle Rafik
(m. 3 children)
Anatoly Kotov
Sofia Kotov
Ludmilla Kovov

Uncle Vladimir
(m. 2 children)
Denis Kotov
Sergei Kotov

(43) Breakthrough

"I found out that Dmitry takes his orders from a person named Sergei," said Aurelia to Parker during their next phone call. "We need to find out information about this Sergei."

"That's fantastic because I discovered that Sergei Kotov is a cousin of Vera Kotov. Vera is married to Lieutenant Cambe," answered Parker.

"Great, you've given me Sergei's last name! We'll now get a handle on Sergei Kotov. We already know that Barry Snyder is connected to the Lieutenant because they each married a Kotov sister. There's evidence that Barry is some sort of carrier of information between the United States and the Soviet Union whenever he plays in a European chess tournament. The next time he travels there, we'll have a tail on him. We'll also start round the clock surveillance of both Sergei and Lieutenant Cambe. We'll see if we can document any contact between the two of them. Parker, I think each of us finding out about Sergei Kotov may be the breakthrough we needed!" Aurelia's voice showed she was excited. Parker, in turn, smiled that his insight where he and Aurelia would jointly work together to solve Oscar's murder was factually now a step closer in reality.

Meanwhile, Vera Kotov Cambe was writing daily letters to various people. The CIA started intercepting them in order to review their contents before forwarding them to the addressed parties. One of the letters was addressed to Barry Snyder saying two electronic devices were ready in Reykjavik, which was a safer place to retrieve them rather than sending them to Barry's home in Chicago; however, Barry had to move quickly because the chess match was nearing a conclusion. Fischer continued to lead Spassky by 3 points and now the chess games were being drawn, which was good for Bobby because the match had only 24 scheduled games, and Fischer was closing in on the 12.5 points necessary to win the match.

Having received Vera's letter, Barry and his wife announced a week's vacation in Iceland and flew to Reykjavik on Friday night August 25, presumably to see the end of the match and Fischer's victory, which happened on Friday, September 1, 1972, when Spassky resigned the adjourned game from the prior night. By that time, Barry had collected the two electronic devices and was ready to return home with his wife tagging along.

Another letter from Vera, this time to her cousin, Sergei, told him that Barry would return from Iceland and would have two devices. They looked harmless and would easily clear customs. They were specialized tape recorders and made to record dolphin whistles and clicks, converting those sounds to English words or letters. The Lieutenant then wrote at the bottom of the note: 'see that the new electronic equipment is used immediately and report results daily'. With this message, Jenkins had evidence of Cambe's direct written involvement in the electronic translator project. He was overjoyed and ordered the final details of the Lieutenant's arrest as a spy for the Soviet Union.

At the same time, Jenkins wanted evidence that Oscar's murderer was Michael Klossmeier, and he had been paid money by Gary Cambe for that murder. It was likely that if the police got evidence that Michael Klossmeier murdered Oscar, then Mic would confess that Cambe was the person who hired him to do the murder. The results of the tests on Mic's knife that had been procured by Marsha showed that although it was free of any traces of blood, that specific knife did produce striations that matched the cut markings on Oscar's neck. The police then purchased ten additional knives of the same type from the same manufacturer and tested them. The striations were very similar to each other for each knife; however, Mic's knife was the closest to Oscar's cuts when one looked long and hard enough using high resolution magnification. Jenkins felt that these cut markings on Oscar's neck were not conclusive because the testing of each knife showed only very small differences, and he sensed that getting a jury of 12 to agree on this highly technical point of knife cuts would be painstaking long and difficult and every juror would have to have perfect vision and patience to see and understand what they were looking at under the microscope.

"We could get three different professors from three different universities to look under the microscope to see if they agree that Mic's knife is the murder weapon," suggested Aurelia.

"Find them and see if they will testify," replied Jenkins convinced that such testimony along with his detailed records would convict Klossmeier, and then Michael's testimony against the Lieutenant would end Gary Cambe's spying.

Meanwhile, Lieutenant Cambe was worried about Michael Klossmeier because Mic's potential girlfriend, Marsha, had left him and Mic was reacting badly. Mic had a new house with the money the Soviet's had sent him for killing Oscar, but unfortunately, he was now drinking excessively because he missed Marsha. The Lieutenant knew about a prostitute who was looking for a change and sent her to Madison Wisconsin with the hope she could get Mic's mind off of

Marsha. Camby had been careful about his own activities, eventually ignoring young women such as Marsha even though he found them desirable because he was committed to the spread of communism in the United States. Camby had eliminated American agents such as Oscar and would continue to help the Soviet Union, but Mic was a potential threat to the Lieutenant's own safety especially if Mic continued drinking and then started talking about his exploits. Cambe knew he would have to keep Mic sober and happy; otherwise, the Lieutenant would have to act to eliminate Mic.

Jim Rowdy continued his surveillance of Mic and noticed that he was now seeing a woman who looked like she had some experience. Apparently, she and Mic didn't hit it off because within two days she returned to Chicago.

"So, Parker, what do you think is going on with Mic?' asked Jim after reporting the arrival and quick departure of the woman.

"Unfortunately, Jim, his split with Marsha, and now a really quick breakup with another woman could be bad news for Mic. He has a new house, but nothing in Mic's experience allows him to enjoy it and to fix the place up to his own liking. He's upset that Marsha left him and now even a new woman didn't help. My guess is that this latest lady was sent to Mic by the Lieutenant. He's worried that if Mic starts drinking himself silly that his murder of Oscar will eventually come to light, and then Cambe's involvement as a Soviet spy will be exposed."

"So, the bad news for Mic is that you think the Lieutenant will have him killed?" said Jim.

"Yes, and thus the question is how will Cambe go about having that murder done? This time he's likely to take a more professional route rather than hiring an amateur as he did with Klossmeier."

"Yes, but that could be dangerous to his career if he hired a professional killer, let's say through organized crime. They would have him in their net," replied Jim. "Additionally, he didn't attempt to get a professional killer to take out Oscar. He got the job done with an amateur.

"That's true, but I was thinking he might have his own policemen try to arrest Mic, possibly even for Oscar's murder, and then Mic would be killed because he tried to avoid capture by the police."

"Yes, I see what you mean. There are many different ways that Mic could be silenced. What should we do?"

"The CIA is now monitoring the Lieutenant. I'll discuss this with Aurelia. I'm comfortable that she and the CIA will come up with a plan as they seem to be very good at that."

(44) Dmitry's Distress

Barry Snyder wrapped the two pieces of electronic equipment in heavy burlap, purchased a box at the main Chicago post office, and stored the devices there waiting for Sergei. On the day that Sergei arrived, Barry was waiting at a White Castle restaurant eating a hamburger. He did not wait long, and Sergei as he passed Barry's table nonchalantly reached down and took the key off the table. Later that day, Sergei was on a Miami bound train carrying the electronic devices in a burlap bag.

Late the next morning, Sergei arrived at the train station and called Dmitry's house. "I'll be taking a cab and will be at your house in a few minutes. I'm delivering the two electronic devices for your use, Comrade Dmitry." Dmitry was taken by surprise, but the call gave him just enough time to straighten things out at his place and close his bedroom door. He was thankful for that, but Sergei annoyed him, and it was difficult for Dmitry to call him a Comrade when addressing him. Dmitry wanted Sergei to go and stay away.

"How is everything going Comrade Dmitry?" asked Sergei carrying the electronic devices as he entered the house.

"We're under pressure here, Comrade Sergei. I hope these electronic devices will speed up our work. Boris has been back out in the ocean and has reestablished contact with the dolphins, including Alpha and Beta." Dmitry now realized that Sergei wasn't going away.

"That's good news Comrade. I'm quite certain, based on the paperwork and explanations that our Comrades in Moscow have supplied with these electronic translators, that your work translating the dolphin voices will speed up significantly. I will leave you to experiment with the electronic translator and get Boris familiar with this device as quickly as possible. Before I go, do you have any updates for me about what's going on here in Miami? For example, have you or Boris figured out the identity of this new agent D that the Americans have?

"No, but we believe Agent D killed our Comrade Gorky Genkin. Is there some way our chief Comrade in Chicago or those in Moscow can help us find the identity of this new agent?" said Dmitry. "Gorky's murder has unnerved both Boris and me." Dmitry now realized that *he, Dmitry, would have to go away to be free of all this.*

"It's been suggested that Aurelia Qundo is agent D," said Sergei. "She apparently is a key player next to Jenkins at the CIA and is very bright. Additionally, both D and Aurelia appeared on the scene recently. Tell me, Comrade Dmitry, is Miss Qundo an agent D possibility?"

"No, Comrade Sergei, Aurelia and I go back years when we were studying at Auburn and we both continue to have similar academic interests in cetaceans. I can tell you without hesitation that she's not a professional assassin."

Sergei continued, "One of my assignments, just for your information, Comrade Dmetri, is to kill agent D. Since agent D killed Comrade Gorky, we cannot ignore his death, and agent D must die under the rules of our cold war so tell me more about this warehouse where Agent D might rendezvous."

Dmitri was now completely appalled by Sergei and desperately wanted him to leave. He quickly said, "The rumor is that the Americans including Agent D use the abandoned warehouse on the Intercostal Waterway as a place to rendezvous. If you drive on the northbound expressway, you will see the warehouse. Take a right at the next exit and then another right and you're there. You'll be able to walk around the place. Generally, there are never many people around, especially when it gets dark. You'll need a strong large flashlight if you enter the open warehouse at night, and you have to be careful because a portion of the intercostal waterway flows through the warehouse. Apparently, Jenkins was once spotted there, which is why the place is thought to be a rendezvous location for the capitalists. If any of this is true, then certainly agent D is involved with the dolphin project because Jenkins certainly is."

"Thank you, Comrade Dmitry, but my time is very limited and I've not a moment to waste. I would be checking out this abandoned warehouse if I definitely knew that it's a rendezvous spot for the Americans and Agent D. Are you absolutely certain that Agent D uses the warehouse to rendezvous?"

Finally, Dmitry became *visibly* annoyed at Sergei, and he replied sternly, "I'm certain my facts are accurate; I tell you Agent D uses the warehouse. I was told this by a person who works for the CIA. Why do you sit here questioning me? Check it out yourself! Our entire Florida operation may be in jeopardy!"

Dmitry was now physically sweating, and Sergei nodded grimly at this harsh warning. The two comrades sat facing each other alone in Dmitry's living room, but Sergei sensed the presence of someone else who listened out of sight behind the closed bedroom door. He decided it was a woman and that he was no longer welcome here. He had interrupted something, and now Dmitry was very angry. Sergei knew that he had to leave Dmitry's house.

"I'm going, Comrade Dmitry, but first, I'm hoping that you can give me a photograph or a description of agent D. I do not know his name or what he looks like. I only know that he is called 'agent D'. It is difficult to kill such an unknown. Why, he may even be a 'she' said Comrade Sergei.

Dmitry was momentarily taken aback by these remarks but replied evenly, "I sympathize with you, Comrade Sergei, but I do not know anything more about agent D. His identity is a mystery, and American intelligence judiciously guards his secret at the highest levels. D may be our most dangerous adversary, not only because he is unknown, but also because he somehow discovered our dolphins. How much he knows I can only guess."

During this last exchange Dmitry began to pace the room, and the sweat on his face was now noticeable. His voice turned solemn as he continued, "I think we're all in great danger as long as D remains unknown. True, I suppose agent D may be a woman as you just implied. Anyway, you must be prepared for any eventuality. That's why it's important to wait at the warehouse and see who shows up since we don't know who D is or what he looks like."

"Very well, I'll go to the warehouse and wait for agent D," replied Sergei. The two comrades stiffly saluted each other, and Sergei left the house. Outside, the cab that Sergei had been waiting for was parked in the driveway. The taxi driver leaned against the hood and looked sadly up at the sky, shaking his head at the lack of rain, "Do you think it's finally going to rain?" asked Sergei, making idle conversation.

“I hope so,” replied the driver with a British accent. “Blimey, this drought has gone on too long. The water table at my place has fallen so low that salt from the ocean is flowing into the well. I don’t know what we are going to do if it doesn’t rain soon.” The cab driver was so agitated by the drought that in backing the cab out of the driveway he nearly crashed into a white Mercedes parked at the curb.

Upon leaving Dmitry’s house, Sergei went immediately to the warehouse where he waited in silence. He waited all day and even when night time arrived with darkness, Sergei continued his watch. The old warehouse was deserted and dilapidated. Deleterious fumes emanated from decaying wooden cartons while rats twittered among the putrid contents. Discolored moonlight filtered through a broken skylight casting grotesque shadows along the filth. The warehouse had been used in the past by boats to load and unload supplies. A large inside wharf faced the Intracoastal Waterway. Sergei Kotov stalked along the pier listening to the passing boats, but none of them stopped.

Sergei remembered the last man he had shot and killed. He had surprised him, caught him off guard, as he was planning to do to agent D. Cruelty and strength transfigured Sergei’s face in anticipation as he held his favorite Makarov pistol in his right hand ready to fire it in an instant. Fortunately, no one came to break Sergei’s lonely vigil on this particular night.

(45) Dmitry Flees

After Sergei left Dmitry's house, the bedroom door opened and Aurelia Qundo emerged. She had arrived early for their weekly lunch and then there was a surprise call from Sergei that he had arrived and was coming over in a cab from the train station. Dmitry straightened up the kitchen and living room, removing any trace of Aurelia, while she hid in the bedroom, closing the door and removing a derringer from her purse just in case Sergei became suspicious and burst through the door. It would not be good for anyone, including the CIA, if she had to use the weapon to defend herself, and she said a prayer that Sergei would leave quickly and then followed it up with a thank you prayer as the cab returned and took him away. She smiled – her parents had taught her correctly the importance to always pray and the importance to recognize that a thank you prayer should follow. All too often people who pray do not follow it up with a thank you prayer as Aurelia did that day.

Unfortunately, the tension for Dmitry of Sergei's surprise visit had taken its toll, and he now sat on the couch with tears forming in his eyes. "What are we doing, Aurelia? Sergei has a gun and is looking to kill someone to even the score for Gorky' death. This is madness …just plain crazy madness. This cold war between America and the Soviets will end in the death of millions. I never should have gotten involved as I did, and now we are drawing in another species. Friendly dolphins are going to be drawn into our wars and deaths given the electronic devices on my kitchen table. These are electronic instruments of death! Mankind using such devices will be communicating with dolphins, and they, another part of nature, will now join this absurd cold war!" Dmitry stopped talking but emotionally his turmoil continued, and his eyes remained moist. Aurelia sat on the couch next to him, waiting for Dmitry's internal storm to pass, which it did.

"What do you want to do Dmitry?" she finally asked after he settled down.

"I can't do this anymore. I'm going to resign from the communist party and give up this apartment. I've been praying and now I want to get away from this world and begin praying in earnest. I've been looking for a monastery, and I think I've found one. Will you be telling your CIA friends about me?"

"I don't think that will be necessary, Dmitry. We know Sergei and his Soviet bosses, and we'll stop them. However, I think you have to leave quickly. Just pack a suitcase and leave."

Dmitry looked at Aurelia and his eyes again became moist, but he stopped short of crying. He nodded agreement. Aurelia stood up. She had made her decision. "I'm going now, Dmitry. If you're leaving Miami, I think you should do so immediately – don't wait – leave tonight!"

Dmitry stood up and the two hugged, "God bless you, Aurelia."

"God bless, you, Dmitry," replied Aurelia who found the change that had happened inside Dmitry ironic. The thought that innocent dolphins were being drawn into human inequities was his tipping point. The fact that such inequities already existed for humans had not been enough. The voices of the dolphins had led him to search for the voices of God.

(46) Cambe Makes a Bad Move

There was a Labor Day party in the Chicago neighborhood where Mic once lived. Mic drove his Studebaker down from Madison to join in the festivities, which were taking place one block from where Delia Dempsey and her daughter Marsha lived and where Mic had once resided. Mic was happy being surrounded by his old buddies: Skip, Bruno, and Big Steve. Skip asked him how the Studebaker was running, and Mic said it was in great shape and thanked Skip for the work he had on it. Bruno asked him about his new house and reminded Mic that if he ever needed work done on the place, he would be happy to make the drive to Madison to help Mic. Big Steve was interested in the financing of the house and was surprised and impressed to learn that Mic had no need of a mortgage because he had enough money to buy the house outright. Marsha had mailed Mic a note, saying she was working as a waitress Labor Day but wanted to see him as soon as she got home. The two had not communicated since Marsha's last visit where it became clear that she was not interested in him, and they had departed leaving Mic discouraged and days of heavy drinking.

Mic saw her arrive and she waved to him as she entered her house. He waited a few minutes and then went to her door which she opened. He was surprised to see a golden-haired woman seated on the couch and two men in suits standing off to side. Marsha said, "These are friends, Michael, and they want to talk to you. All is good. I'll be waiting outside," and then with a smile to Mic, she stepped out of the house, closing the door behind her.

"I'm Parker Spooner, Mr. Klossmeier, and this lady is Miss Aurelia Qundo. Please sit next to her." Mic was confused and knew something was wrong. The beautiful golden-haired woman calmed him slightly as he sat next to her, but the other man who wasn't introduced was tall and well built. He stood by the door observing. Mic instinctively knew that he had a gun under his suit coat. Mic was correct - he did have a gun because he was a Federal Marshall working directly with the Commissioner who ran the Chicago Police Department. Parker pulled up a chair to the coffee table and faced Mic and Aurelia, who sat on the couch on the other side of the table.

"You can call me, Aurelia, Mr. Klossmeier, and here are my credentials." She showed him her CIA badge. "We are here to prevent your assassination. You'll be murdered if you go outside."

Mic turned pale. He turned his head back and forth, looking at the hulking man at the door, Parker across the table, and the golden hair woman with the badge. He almost jumped up to flee or to grab Aurelia but went cold when he heard 'prevent your assassination". He stammered, "What do you mean by my assassination?"

Parker continued, "Darkness is approaching and under instructions from Lieutenant Gary Cambe police units are surrounding this block to arrest you for the murder of Oscar Busby. Cambe has conveyed to his officers that you, Michael Klossmeier, are armed and dangerous. As Mic the Knife, you almost certainly have your knife on you, and you almost certainly will wind up dead when you attempt to flee or resist arrest." Parker paused to allow this information to register.

Michael sank lower into the couch, "Cambe is going to arrest me for murdering Oscar. That's unbelievable!"

“Not really, Michael, you see the Lieutenant is a Russian spy,” said Aurelia. “He hired you to kill Oscar. You didn’t realize that Oscar was a CIA agent and that he was going to name Gary Cambe as a Russian spy. You were innocent of all that stuff, but now we’re closing in on the Lieutenant as a Russian spy, and your testimony that he hired you to kill a CIA agent will finish him. With your testimony against the Lieutenant, you will likely lighten your sentence and avoid the death penalty for murdering Oscar Busby.”

“Let me look outside,” said Michael standing up. The Federal Marshall put up one hand for Michael to stop and opening the front door with his other hand, he asked Marsha, who was standing outside by the door, to come inside and go into one of the back rooms.

“Marsha, do you know what’s going on? Are there Chicago cops out there?” cried Michael.

“I don’t know what’s going on, Mic,” replied Marsha running by him into the back bedroom where Delia was hiding, “but yes, many Chicago police cars pulled up a few minutes ago and have surrounded the entire block.”

Michael Klossmeier went to the front door and looked out, standing next to the Federal Marshall who now had his free hand on his hidden gun. The Labor Day crowd was still there, but now there were several police cars on each end of the block, red lights were flashing, as the crowd was being pushed back by policemen who were preparing to search the area. Mic quickly retreated from the door and slumped back into the couch. This was similar to the time when he had just turned 18 and had stabbed a guy. The cops caught him and so he went to jail for a short period of time. Now he had killed a man for money, and he was going back to jail likely for the rest of his life. The heavy-set detective read Mic his Miranda rights and gave him a paper which said Michael Klossmeier had killed Oscar and received money from Gary Cambe for the crime. Mic read the paper, said it was all true, and began to curse Camby and then himself for stupidity. Mic signed the paper and Heavy Set went to the telephone to notify the Commissioner. A few minutes later, the Chicago police stopped their search and left the area. Aurelia said goodbye to Parker in order to catch a CIA plane back to Miami. The two of them smiled at each other. Parker bowed slightly to Aurelia, and she in turn returned the bow. They had done it: Mic the Knife who killed Oscar Busby was arrested and in custody, and the man who ordered his killing, the Russian spy and police officer, Lieutenant Gary Cambe, was about to be arrested.

(47) Justice for All

Lieutenant Cambe spent an anxious Labor Day night waiting for a telephone call that never came. He was expecting a call that Mic had resisted arrest and had been killed. No call meant that he had somehow avoided the police and wasn't arrested. Cambe went to bed with the hope that the attempted arrest and murder would now happen overnight. If Mic was arrested but still alive, Cambe would have figure out a way to kill him and do it quickly before Mic figured out that he had been doubled crossed. If Mic was alive and free, then Cambe would have to design a plan to have him killed. But none of this happened because early the next morning the Lieutenant and his wife were shocked when the Commissioner's police came to his house to arrest the Lieutenant for hiring Michael Klossmeire to murder Oscar Busby.

That very morning Jenkins in Miami contacted agents Stein and Watts and told them to get their teams together for the impending arrests of two Russian spies. He had Miss Qundo and Williams obtain from a court Judge arrest warrants that had already been prepared for Dmitry Doby and Boris Volkov. Williams was writing notes to himself and paused. "What should we do about the dolphins?" he suddenly asked.

"I'll ask agent D to handle the situation," said Jenkins. A faraway look crossed his eyes. "Yes, agent D will know what to do about the dolphins," he said softly and then added, "Also what do we know about this other Russian operative, Sergei Kotov?"

"Not very much," replied Williams, "He appears to be some sort of hit man and organizer. He travels back and forth between the States and Europe, probably carrying information. My guess is that once we arrest Boris and Dmitry, Sergei will try to flee and go underground."

"That wouldn't be good" opined Jenkins, "however, it's more important for us to break up the communication between Boris and Dmitry and to arrest both of them. We'll do that this afternoon. I'll alert D who should be able to handle Sergei before he escapes."

Later that afternoon, Boris was shopping and squeezed a tomato as he picked it out of its carton. "I'll take these six," he said to a clerk, a stout man with a pleasant face. A large sign covered the wall in the grocery store: FRESH FRUITS AND VEGETABLES, FREE FROM DDT SPRAYING. The clerk priced the tomatoes and placed them in a brown paper bag and attached a receipt as Boris gave him the money for the purchase. Boris walked down one of the aisles in the busy store and from his pocket nonchalantly transferred a dolphin tape to the ubiquitous brown bag. Dmitry would soon be along to pick up that tape and the recent purchase. At the end of the aisle, he found an empty shopping cart and judicially parked it and carefully placed the paper bag into the cart. Free of his purchase, Boris left the grocery store.

Outside, a taxicab driver bumped into him and two other men surrounded him. The driver flashed an American CIA badge but spoke with a British accent, "Don't make a scene, mate, you're under arrest for spying for a foreign power – just get into the cab." With that the two men pushed him into the back seat, one on each side, and agent Watts got into the cab and drove away.

Inside, agent Stein waited for Dmitry Doby to go to the shopping cart that Boris had just set up and then abandoned. Dmitry would normally have picked up the paper bag, making certain that the tape was inside next to the tomatoes and that the receipt was attached. Then Dmitry would have turned around and exited the grocery store through a side door. At that point he would have been stopped on the sidewalk by two men, and the stout clerk with a pleasant face would have come from behind holding a badge and agent Stein would have made the arrest. But none of that happened because Dmitry Doby didn't show up at the grocery store. Dmitry had already left Miami.

Later that day, Jenkins lit a cigarette and leaned back in his chair, looking at Miss Qundo and debating his opening words, but she started, "We have a report that Sergei is at the warehouse. We should send agents before he kills someone."

"No," replied Jenkins, "D is going to handle Sergei." The smoke from his cigarette hung ominously in the air. Jenkins coughed.

"Sir, you really should give up smoking. It's harming your health." She said it as a matter of fact, suppressing her emotion that she was in love with this man.

"Living is harming my health," growled Jenkins, "Man is an inveterate polluter and probably incorrigible." He crushed the cigarette in an ash tray and looked closely at her. Miss Qundo never believed Jenkins when he talked this way – she knew and understood him – this act was just part of how he handled the pressure of his position.

Special agent Jenkins continued, "Anyway I want to congratulate you on your work in exposing your college classmate, Dmitry Doby, and his spying. Ending his work with Boris Volkov was important for us, and you also worked with Dmitry while he was doing dolphin research and all of that could not have been easy for you. I imagine that's why you alerted him to his upcoming arrest, which allowed Dmitry to escape."

Aurelia was surprised that Jenkins knew this and immediately wondered why he hadn't stopped her or Dmitry's escape. She quickly regained her composer and answered, "Dmitry's a naïve scientist and is finished with communism and possibly the modern world. He cried after Sergei left his apartment because Sergei said he was going to kill agent D to avenge the death of Gorky. Dmitry Doby is no longer a spy or a Soviet agent and only got involved because his parents raised him to believe that communism was good. Dealing with people like Sergei showed him reality and turned him off of communism. Dmitry is no longer a danger to the United States."

"Then you didn't allow him to flee because you fell in love with him?"

"No, sir," said Aurelia emphatically. "He needs a mother's love, … *not the love that a woman like me can give.*"

"What if it turns out that your judgment that he's harmless and no longer acting as a Soviet spy turns out to be incorrect?"

"I should be fired, dealt with according to CIA procedures, and then the CIA would have to deal with Dmitry accordingly."

"Before all of this happened, I was recommending a promotion for you – there's an opening at Langley, and you would be perfect for it."

Miss Qundo shook her head in doubt, her golden hair moving gently around her shoulders, "I don't know about that, sir. Besides, isn't that all academic at this point? You're not recommending me any longer because I allowed Dmitry to run away."

Jenkins quickly responded to the contrary, "Langley is a natural step for you, Miss Qundo. You have the talent for their work. Initially, you risked your life working with your former college classmate when it wasn't known if he was dangerous or not. You do belong at Langley, and I would recommend you … if … *if ... you decide you really want to go to Langley."*

Jenkins paused. Aurelia did not move but quietly continued to look at him with a look that showed she loved him. The words she had said a few moments ago gave him hope and now her unmistakable look of love the certainty he needed. She had deliberately said *'not the love that a woman like me can give.'* He leaned forward and Frank Jenkins slowly and with meaning responded to her, "*However, if you do go, I shall truly miss you, Miss Qundo."*

Miss Qundo's heart jumped, catching Jenkins with a different tone of voice. She knew when he said 'I will truly miss you, Miss Qundo' it was done in a very special way, conveying finally for the first time in an unmistaken manner that she was a woman and that he was a man who loved her.

Her face acknowledged both him and his intent as she leaned forward. Their eyes locked together and their minds understood each other. "I would also miss you, sir, and thus, I don't want to move to Langley. I wish to stay here with … *with you.*"

"That's wonderful because I'm in love with you, Miss Qundo!"

"And I have loved you for a long time and have waited for those words, Frank!"

Frank stood up and went to Aurelia. "Aurelia," he said using her first name and taking her in his arms to kiss her lips.

Given the order, grace, and structure of reality, when true love is acknowledged, hope arises, and happiness follows.

(48) Agent D and the Aftermath

Sergei heard a noise. It was a faint, distant sound, but it came from inside the warehouse – perhaps from the wharf. Cautiously, he moved in that direction with his gun arm poised and his finger on the trigger. The noise came from underneath the pier. It sounded like something was gently rubbing against the wood. There were no boats anywhere in the water as Sergei came to the edge of the wharf. Glancing down, he saw that a black oil slick clung to the surface of the once azure water like an amorphous parasite.

Below the water level and oil slick, the sonar of a large dolphin mapped Sergei's physical and emotional states and within an instant the enormous mammal leaped vertically completely out of the water and twirled in mid-air sweeping its tail across the pier. The powerful blow against Sergei's body discharged the gun harmlessly into the wharf and swept him into the murky waters below. There, Sergei had no chance against Agent D and drowned.

Agent D had already stopped his fellow dolphins from spying, and thus Jenkins closed the file, marking it Highly Sensitive – Classified.

Later that month Frank Jenkins and Aurelia Qundo married each other in Father Joseph's church in front of a large congregation of relatives and friends. Parker and Rosemary Spooner and their four children were in the audience that witnessed the marriage.

"Church weddings are so beautiful," said a happy Grace to her sister, Anna, who was seated next to her. Anna looked up to her big sister and whispered, "Someday that's going to be you, Grace, getting married, and I'll be standing next to you as the maid of honor." Peter seated next to them had been mentally computing a variation in the Petroff Defense and had to focus extra hard on the imaginary chess board in front of him once the whispering of his sisters started. Meanwhile, John was thinking about Marie, a girl that was a classmate of his at the University of Chicago and wondering why he had been afraid of asking her to go with him to the wedding.

Parker and Rosemary sat together holding hands, smiling as they watched the wedding with their four children. Quietly, Rosemary and Parker had renewed their marriage vows.

www.ingramcontent.com/pod-product-compliance
Lightning Source LLC
LaVergne TN
LVHW052336100826
845147LV00020B/1074